W9-CKL-550

By Janet Evanovich

The Stephanie Plum Novels

Explosive Eighteen

Smokin' Seventeen

Sizzling Sixteen

Finger Lickin' Fifteen

Fearless Fourteen

Lean Mean Thirteen

Twelve Sharp

Eleven on Top

Ten Big Ones

To the Nines

Hard Eight

Seven Up

Hot Six

High Five

Four to Score

Three to Get Deadly

Two for the Dough

One for the Money

The Between the Numbers Novels

Plum Spooky

Plum Lucky

Plum Lovin'

Visions of Sugar Plums

The Lizzy and Diesel Novels

Wicked Business

Wicked Appetite

The Barnaby and Hooker Novels

Trouble Maker
(graphic novel)

Motor Mouth

Metro Girl

Nonfiction

How I Write

WICKED BUSINESS

WICKED BUSINESS

A Lizzy and Diesel Novel

JANET EVANOVICH

DOUBLEDAY LARGE PRINT HOME LIBRARY EDITION

BANTAM BOOKS NEW YORK

This Large Print Edition, prepared especially for Doubleday Large Print Home Library, contains the complete, unabridged text of the original Publisher's Edition.

Published in the United States by Bantam Books, an imprint of The Random House Publishing Group, a division of Random House, Inc., New York.

BANTAM BOOKS and the rooster colophon are registered trademarks of Random House, Inc.

ISBN 978-1-62090-032-1

Printed in the United States of America

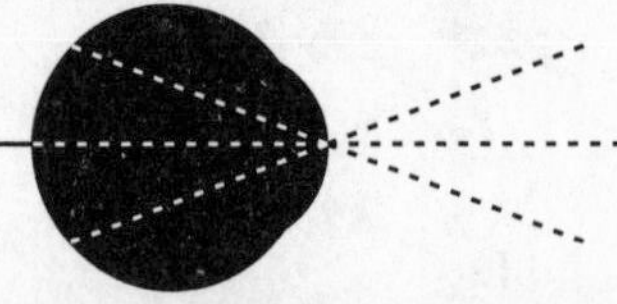

This Large Print Book carries the Seal of Approval of N.A.V.H.

WICKED BUSINESS

CHAPTER ONE

My name is Lizzy Tucker, and I used to think I was normal. My hair is blond with some chemical assistance. My eyes are brown from my Grandpa Harry. I'm 5'5" tall, and my breasts measure more than my waist so I'm a happy camper. I had a mildly embarrassing childhood free from any truly significant disasters. I wasn't a cheerleader or the prom queen. I didn't graduate with honors. I chose culinary school after high school, where I limped my way through butchering beasts and excelled at baking cakes. I was engaged and disengaged. Good riddance to him. In January, three days after my twenty-eighth birthday, I inherited a house from my Great Aunt Ophelia, and I took a job as pastry chef at Dazzle's Bakery in Salem.

For five terrific months, I felt like my life was finally coming together. And then two men and a monkey dropped into my world and changed it forever.

One of the men is called Wulf, short for Gerwulf Grimoire. He's eerily handsome, with midnight black, shoulder-length hair that waves over his ears. His skin is pale, his eyes are dark, and his intentions are even darker. The other guy is big and scruffy, and beach bum blond. He has a hard muscled body, a questionable attitude, and a monkey named Carl. The big, scruffy guy is unexplainably charming, and he has only one name . . . Diesel.

The men are my age. And according to Diesel, we're part of a loosely organized band of humans with abilities beyond the ordinary. I don't entirely believe all this, but I don't disbelieve it, either. I recognize that some people are smarter, braver, stronger, can sing better, are luckier than others. So who's to say some people don't have abilities just north of normal. I mean, it's not like he's telling me he's Superman from the planet Krypton, right?

This is my first October in New England. I still love my job and Ophelia's small, two-bedroom saltbox that sits on the crest of a hill overlooking Marblehead Harbor. The house was built in 1740 and over the years has had some renovation, with varying degrees of success. It's a little lopsided and the windows aren't plumb, but it has a working fireplace, and from day one it's felt like home.

Usually, I work from five in the morning until one in the afternoon, but today I had the day off. Rain was slanting against my kitchen windows, and the ancient maple in my backyard rattled in the wind. I was in the middle of chopping vegetables for soup when my back door blew open and Diesel stepped into my tiny mudroom. He was wearing motorcycle boots, washed-out jeans, a

T-shirt that advertised beer, and an unzipped gray sweatshirt. He had a two-day beard, his hair was thick and unruly and wet from the rain, and he was sex walking.

"I need you to come with me," Diesel said. "Some guy just got pitched off his fourth-floor balcony, and Wulf is involved. There's a rumor going around that Wulf's got a lead on another SALIGIA Stone. I imagine this murder fits in somehow."

The story Diesel tells is that seven ancient stones hold the power of the seven deadly sins. They're called the Stones of SALIGIA, and if you combine them in the same vessel you get really bad juju going . . . like hell on earth. Some people believe the stones have found their way to Salem. Wulf happens to be one of those people, and he's made it known that he wants them. Since Wulf is thought to inhabit the dark side from time to time, Diesel has been bestowed the responsibility of preventing him from collecting the stones.

"Ordinarily, I wouldn't mind tagging

along," I said to Diesel, "but I'm making soup."

"Okay, let's take a look at what we've got. You can stay here and make soup, or you can go with me and save mankind from getting chucked into Satan's stew pot."

I blew out a sigh. Having special abilities sounds good on paper. And there are some people, like Wulf, who might enjoy the power those abilities bring, but I found the gift to be an awkward burden. I get that someone has to save mankind from the big stew pot in hell, but why *me*?

"To tell you the truth, I've never really bought into the whole SALIGIA thing," I said to Diesel. "And I truly don't feel equipped to save mankind."

"You have a critical ability I lack," Diesel said. "You're one of only two people who can sense objects related to the SALIGIA Stones."

"And you think I'll have to use that ability at this crime scene?"

"Probably not," Diesel said, "but you're cute. And if I have to go look at some idiot who face-planted onto the side-walk in the rain, I'm taking you with me."

"You think I'm cute?"

"Yeah. Can you hurry it up here, please?"

It's sort of alarming that I can be so easily swayed by a compliment, but there you have it. I scooped the chopped vegetables into my soup pot and clapped a lid on it. I grabbed my purse off the kitchen counter, snatched a hooded sweatshirt off a peg next to the door, and stepped outside.

The cloud cover was low, the rain was turning to a drizzle, and there was a chill in the air. There were still boats on moorings in the harbor below my house, but their number was significantly decreased from the summer crush. It was definitely fall in New England.

Diesel opened the white picket fence gate that led from my small backyard to the alley where he was illegally parked. He was driving a red Jeep Grand Cherokee that wasn't new and wasn't old. Usually, it was mud-splattered and coated in road dust. Today, the rain had washed the top layer of dirt away and it looked almost clean.

I slid onto the passenger-side seat, buckled myself in, and realized Carl was in the back. Carl looked up at me, gave me a finger wave, and smiled a horrible monkey smile. All monkey gums and monkey teeth and crazy bright monkey eyes.

I grew up in suburbia. We had cats, dogs, hamsters, guinea pigs, parakeets, and fish. Never a monkey. A monkey was a new, sometimes disturbing experience.

Diesel drove down Weatherby Street to Pleasant, Pleasant turned into Lafayette, and Lafayette took us to the bridge that crossed into Salem. We followed traffic through the center of town, cut off to the north side, parked behind a police cruiser on Braintree Street, and made our way over to where a small crowd was gathering.

This was a mixed neighborhood of commercial and residential. Cop cars, a truck belonging to the medical examiner, and an EMT truck were angle parked in front of a seven-story, yellow brick condo building that looked like it had been built in the seventies. Crime scene tape cordoned off an area in front of the building, and a makeshift screen had been erected, preventing gawkers like me from seeing the body sprawled on the rain-slicked pavement. Thank heaven for the screen. I didn't want to see the dead guy.

"Do you know his name?" I asked Diesel.

"Gilbert Reedy. He's a professor at Harvard. My source tells me Reedy came flying through the air and crash landed with a handprint burned into his neck."

I felt my breakfast roll in my stomach, and my upper lip broke out in a sweat. "Oh boy," I said. "Damn."

Diesel looked down at me. "Breathe. And think about something else."

"How can I think about something else? There's a dead man on the ground, and he has a handprint burned into his flesh."

"Think about baseball," Diesel said.

"Okay, baseball. Am I playing or watching?"

"You're watching."

"Am I at the park? Or is it on television?"

"Television."

Diesel tipped his head back and looked up at a shattered slider, leading to a postage-stamp-size balcony on the fourth floor. I looked up, too.

"I know of only one person who can channel enough energy to leave a burn mark like that on someone's neck," Diesel said.

"Wulf?"

"Yes."

"So you think Wulf pitched Reedy through the window and off the balcony?"

"Everything points to that, but it would be out of character for Wulf. Wulf likes things neat. And this is messy. I can't see Wulf throwing a guy out a window . . . especially in the rain."

"That would be more *you*," I said.

"Yeah. That would be more *me*."

I scanned the crowd on the other side of the crime scene and spotted Wulf. He was standing alone, and he was impeccably dressed in black slacks and sweater. He didn't look like a man who not so long ago threw someone out a window. His hair was swept back, and his dark eyes were focused on me with an intensity that made my skin prickle.

I felt Diesel move closer, his body touching mine, his hand at my neck. A protective posture. Wulf nodded in acknowledgment. There was a flash of light, some smoke, and when the smoke cleared, Wulf was gone.

"He's been doing the smoke thing ever since he went to magic camp in the third grade," Diesel said. "It's getting old. He really needs to get some new parlor tricks."

Diesel and Wulf are cousins. They're related by blood, but separated by temperament and ideology. Diesel works as a kind of bounty hunter for the regulatory agency that keeps watch over humans with exceptional abilities. Wulf is just Wulf. And from what I'm told, that's almost never good.

"Now what?" I asked Diesel. "Are you going to tell the police?"

"No. That's not the way we do things. Wulf is my responsibility."

"Whoops."

"Yeah, I'm behind the curve on this one."

I saw a flash of brown fur scuttle past me, and Carl crawled under the tarp that screened the body.

"I thought you locked him in the car," I said to Diesel.

"I did."

"What the heck?" someone yelled from the other side of the tarp. "Where'd the monkey come from? He's contaminating the crime scene. Somebody call animal control."

Diesel slipped under the tarp and returned with Carl. We hustled back to the car, we all got in, and Diesel took off down the street.

"He's holding something in his hand," I said to Diesel. "It looks like a key."

Carl put it in his mouth and bit down. "Eeee!"

I traded him a mint, and I took the key. It was sized to fit a diary or journal, and it was intricately engraved with tiny vines and leaves.

"Is this yours?" I asked Diesel.

"No. He must have picked it up off the ground."

"Maybe he got it off Reedy. Maybe he snatched it out of his pocket."

"I took a look at Reedy, and he didn't have pockets. He was only wearing boxers and one sock. I guess he could have had the key stuck up his nose or inserted south of the border."

I took hand sanitizer out of my purse and squirted it onto the key. Diesel cut across a couple streets, found Lafayette, and turned toward Marblehead.

"Are we done?" I asked him.

"If we were done, I'd be on a beach in the South Pacific. I thought we'd go back to your house so you can finish your soup and I can do some research on Gilbert Reedy."

CHAPTER TWO

Diesel peeled off Pleasant Street and wound around the historic area of Marblehead, following narrow streets designed for horses and foot traffic. He turned onto Weatherby Street and parked in front of my little house. The clapboards are gray, the trim is white, and there are two onion lamps on either side of my red front door.

Glo was sitting on my stoop with her black sweatshirt hood pulled up and her canvas messenger bag hugged to her chest. She's single, like me. She's four years younger, an inch shorter, and she's the counter girl at Dazzle's. Her curly red hair is chopped into a short bob, and her taste in clothes runs somewhere between Disney Princess and punk rocker. Today she was wearing black Uggs, black tights, a short black skirt, and a black, orange, pink, and baby blue striped knit shirt under the black sweatshirt. She stood when she saw us, and her face lit up with a smile.

"I was afraid you'd never come home, and I'd be stuck out here forever," she said.

I looked up and down the street. "Where's your car?"

"It's back at my apartment. It's leaking something."

"How'd you get here?"

"My neighbor was passing through and dropped me off. I thought you were making soup this morning."

"There was a temporary change in plans," I told her.

Diesel opened my front door, Carl rushed into the house, and we all followed him to the kitchen, where Cat 7143 was perched on a stool. Cat is shorthaired, tiger-striped, has one eye and half a tail. Glo rescued Cat 7143 from the shelter and gave him to me. It said Cat 7143 on his adoption paper, and he's been Cat 7143 ever since. Cat jumped off the stool, sniffed at Carl, and walked away in disgust. Carl flipped him the bird and claimed the stool.

"Put the hex on anybody lately?" Diesel asked Glo.

Glo set her messenger bag on the counter. "No. I tried to put a happy spell on my broom, but it didn't work. He's still cranky."

Glo's read the entire Harry Potter series four times and has aspirations toward wizardry. A couple months ago, she found *Ripple's Book of Spells* in a curio shop, and she's been test-driving spells ever since. I like Glo a lot, and she's an excellent counter girl, but she's a disaster as a wizard.

"What kind of soup are you making?" Glo asked, looking into my pot.

"Vegetable with beef broth and noodles."

"Are you putting any exotic herbs in it? I have some powdered eye of newt with me." Glo rummaged around in her bag and pulled out a small jar. "And I've got lizard eggs, but they might be expired. I got them on sale."

"Thanks," I said, "but I'll pass."

I took the little key out of my pocket, set it on the counter, and went to the sink to wash my hands.

"Omigosh," Glo said. "It's the Lovey key. I didn't realize you were the one who bought the sonnets."

"I didn't buy sonnets," I told her. "I found the key. Technically, Carl found it."

Glo picked the key up and squinted at it. "If you look real close, you can see the *L* inscribed in the middle of the vines. It's absolutely ancient, and Nina at Ye Olde Exotica Shoppe said it might be enchanted. It goes with a little book of sonnets. I was saving up money to buy the book from Nina, but someone beat me to it."

I tied my chef apron around my waist and looked over at Glo. "I didn't realize you liked poetry."

"Nina let me read some of the sonnets. They're so romantic. And some of them are totally bawdy."

"Nothing better than a bawdy sonnet," Diesel said, helping himself to a bagel.

I couldn't imagine Diesel liking a sonnet, bawdy or otherwise. I thought Diesel was more of a limerick kind of guy.

Glo returned the key to the counter. "Nina told me the sonnets were guaranteed to inspire lust, and I thought they might come in handy. You never know when you might want to inspire lust in someone, right?"

I glanced over at Diesel and thought I'd rather have a charm that helped me *ignore* lust.

"I want to do some research on Gilbert Reedy," Diesel said to me. "Is it okay if I use your computer?"

"Sure."

"Who's Gilbert Reedy?" Glo wanted to know.

"Dead guy," Diesel said. "Took a swan dive off his fourth-floor balcony this morning."

I set the dining room table for three. I was serving soup and fresh baked bread for lunch. Oatmeal cookies for dessert.

Diesel ambled in from the living room to join Glo and me, and Carl hopped onto the fourth chair.

"Chee?" Carl asked.

"No," Diesel said. "It's soup. Remember when you had the meltdown over mashed potatoes? Soup is worse."

Carl gave him the finger, jumped off, scurried into the kitchen, and returned with a bowl. He set the bowl on the table and scrambled onto his chair. Too short. He could barely see over the table. He jumped down, ran to the closet, and came back with his booster chair. He climbed onto the booster and smiled his scary monkey smile at everyone. Hopeful.

"Isn't that cute," Glo said. "He wants soup."

I'd seen Carl eat, and I agreed with Diesel. I didn't think soup was a good idea. I put a slice of bread into Carl's bowl and spooned a little broth over it. Carl pointed at my soup and pointed to his bowl. He wanted more.

"Not gonna happen," Diesel said.

Carl threw his bowl onto the floor and glared at Diesel. Diesel blew out a sigh, plucked Carl off the booster seat, carted him to the back door, and pitched him out.

"What if he runs away?" Glo asked.

"Lucky me," Diesel said.

"He's not going to run away," I told Diesel. "He's going to stand out there in the rain until you let him come in, and then the whole house will smell like wet monkey."

There was some scratching at the door, the lock tumbled, the door opened, and Carl stomped past us into the living room. He turned the television on, surfed a couple channels, and settled for the Home Shopping Network. We all rolled our eyes and got busy with our soup.

"Did you find anything interesting on Reedy?" I asked Diesel.

"He taught Elizabethan literature. He was single. Originally from the Midwest. Drove a hybrid. Forty-two years old. No indication that he was exceptional in any way."

"Boy, that's impressive," Glo said. "Do you have to buy into a search program to find that kind of stuff?"

Diesel mopped the last of his soup

up with a crust of bread. "No. It was on his Facebook page. He also had a blog where he wrote about finding a book of sonnets that was said to have magical powers."

Glo went wide-eyed. "I bet he was talking about Lovey's book! Is that where you found the key? Was the key on Gilbert Reedy?"

"Maybe," Diesel said. "Maybe not."

Carl walked into the dining room and mooned Diesel. It lost some impact, since Carl didn't wear pants and his business wasn't new to us.

"Dude," Diesel said. "That's no way to get dessert."

Carl snapped to attention. "Eep?"

"Cookies," I told him.

Carl jumped onto his booster seat, sat ramrod straight, and folded his hands on the table. He was a *good* monkey. I gave him a cookie, and he shoved it into his mouth.

"Manners," Diesel said to him.

Carl spit the cookie out onto the table, picked it up, and carefully nibbled at it.

"I should probably go home," Glo said

when we were done with lunch. "I have to do laundry, and my broom might be lonely." She carried her plates into the kitchen, shrugged into her sweatshirt, and hung her messenger bag on her shoulder. "Thanks for the soup and cookies. I'll see you tomorrow bright and early." She left by the back door, and a moment later, she returned. "I don't have a car," she said. "I forgot."

"No problem," Diesel said. "Lizzy and I were going out anyway. We can take you home."

I raised my eyebrows at Diesel. "We were going out?"

"People to see. Things to do," Diesel said.

Twenty minutes later, we dropped Glo off. Another fifteen minutes, and we were parked in front of Gilbert Reedy's apartment building. A plywood panel covered the shattered fourth-floor patio window. It was the only evidence that a tragedy had occurred. The body had been removed from the pavement. The police cars and EMTs were gone. The crime scene tape was gone. No CSI truck in sight. Rain was still sifting down.

Diesel got out and opened my door. "Let's look around."

"You look around. I'll wait here."

"Doesn't work that way," Diesel said. "We're partners."

"I don't want to be a partner."

"Yeah, and I don't want to live with a monkey."

It was a valid point, so I unhooked my seatbelt and followed him into the lobby. I stepped back when he went to the elevator.

"Whoa," I said. "Where are you going?"

"Reedy lived in 4B."

"You're going to break into his apartment?"

"Yeah."

"That's against the law. And it's icky."

Diesel yanked me into the elevator and pushed the 4 button. "It feels like the right thing to do."

"Not to me."

"You're the junior partner. You only have a fifteen percent vote."

"Why am I the junior partner? I'm just as powerful as you are."

The elevator doors opened onto the

fourth floor, and Diesel shoved me out into the hall. "In your dreams."

"You can find empowered people, and I find empowered objects. That seems pretty equal to me."

"Honey, I have a whole laundry list of enhanced abilities. And let's face it, you make cupcakes."

I felt my mouth drop open.

Diesel grinned down at me. "Would it help if I said they're really great cupcakes?"

"You've eaten your last."

Diesel wrapped an arm around my shoulders and hugged me into him. "You don't mean that." He removed the crime scene tape sealing 4B's door, placed his hand over the dead bolt, and the bolt slid back, demonstrating one of the laundry list abilities. Diesel could unlock *anything*. He turned the knob, we stepped into Reedy's apartment, and Diesel locked the door again.

It was small but comfortably furnished, with an overstuffed couch and two chairs. Large coffee table, loaded with books, a few pens, a stack of papers held together with a giant rubber band. Flat screen television opposite the couch. Desk to the side of the smashed patio door. We peeked into the kitchen. The appliances were old but clean. Small table and two chairs. Coffee mug in the sink. There was one bedroom and one bath. Nothing extraordinary about either.

"What are we doing here?" I asked Diesel.

"Looking for something."

"That narrows it down."

We migrated to the bookcase by Reedy's desk. He had a wide-ranging assortment of classics, some biographies, some historical fiction, and a large poetry collection that took up an entire shelf. Lovey's book wasn't in the collection. I went to Reedy's bedroom and looked around. No book of sonnets. No sonnets in the bathroom or kitchen.

"Nothing seems out of place," I said to Diesel, "but I don't see Lovey's sonnets."

"CSI has already gone through here collecting prints and whatever they think might be useful," Diesel said. "I don't see a cell phone or computer. I guess they could have taken the book, but it doesn't seem likely. They'd have no reason to believe it was important. It's more likely the killer took the book."

I walked to the coffee table and stared down at a Shakespeare anthology that had to weigh at least fourteen pounds. The cover was faded. The pages were dog-eared and yellow with age. A lined legal pad had been used to hold a place in the book. I flipped the book open and scanned the page.

"Reedy has this anthology turned to one of Shakespeare's sonnets," I said to Diesel. "And he'd taken some notes on it. He copied the line *Sometimes too hot the eye of heaven shines* and he wrote *Key to Luxuria Stone* and underlined it twice. And then farther down the page he has a list of professional papers and books. Lovey's book is the last on the list."

Diesel looked over my shoulder at Reedy's notes. "*Luxuria* is Latin for *lust*."

"You can read Latin?"

"Superbia, Acedia, Luxuria, Ira, Gula, Invidia, Avaritia. The seven deadly sins. That's the extent of my Latin."

"Do you think Reedy was killed because he was researching the Luxuria Stone?"

"People have chased after the stones for centuries, going on nothing more than blind faith that the stones exist, and they've done some horrific things to get them. It wouldn't surprise me if Reedy was the latest victim in a long history of victims."

We went silent at the sound of someone trying the doorknob. There was some scratching and jiggling. A pause. More scratching and jiggling. Another pause. Someone was trying to pick the lock and not having any success. Diesel went to the door, peeked out the security peephole, and turned back to me, smiling.

"It was Hatchet," Diesel said. "It looks like he's leaving."

Steven Hatchet is a soft lump of dough with red scarecrow hair. He's sworn allegiance to Wulf, dresses in full Renaissance regalia, and is off-the-chart crazy. He's in his late twenties and is the only other human known to have an ability similar to mine. Supposedly, we can sense energy locked inside common objects. At first glance, it sounds like fantasyland to be able to do this, but I don't imagine it's much different from a farmer using a divining rod to find water underground. Although honestly, I'm not sure I believe in divining rods.

We took one last tour of the apartment, and Diesel scooped up the anthology, the pad, and the folders.

"You can't take all that stuff," I said. "That's stealing."

"Think of it as borrowing," Diesel said. "Someday I might bring them back."

Diesel locked the door and stuck the crime scene tape back in place. We took the elevator to the lobby and ran into Hatchet carrying a chain saw.

"Does Wulf know you're playing with power tools?" Diesel asked Hatchet.

"My lord only knows I will get the job done. He cares not how. You and your slut need not know more than this."

I felt my eyes narrow, and I listed a couple inches in Hatchet's direction. "Slut? Excuse me?"

Diesel slid an arm around my shoulders and eased me far enough back so my fist couldn't reach Hatchet's nose.

"It's not a secret," Diesel said. "Everyone knows Wulf is looking for the Luxuria Stone."

"And we will succeed," Hatchet said. "We have the sonnets, and we will shortly secure the key."

"Why didn't you get the key when you took the sonnets?" Diesel asked.

Hatchet's face flushed red. "It was an oversight." He turned on his heel and marched to the elevator.

"He's going to cut a hole in Reedy's front door with the chain saw," I said to Diesel.

"Not likely," Diesel said. "It's a metal fire door. If Hatchet wants to get in, he's going to have to go through the wall."

CHAPTER THREE

It was pouring rain by the time we got back to my house. We kicked our shoes off in the mudroom and padded sock-footed into the kitchen. Diesel took a couple cookies from the cookie jar.

"You could have defended my honor back there when Hatchet called me your slut," I said to Diesel.

"I was enjoying the moment. I've always wanted a slut of my own."

Carl wandered into the kitchen. He'd been sleeping on the couch in the living room, and he had bed-head monkey fur all over. He scratched his stomach and eyeballed Diesel's cookie. "Eee?"

I gave Carl a cookie and turned my attention to the anthology and the folders Diesel had placed on the counter. The first folder was labeled *General History of the SALIGIA*. The second folder contained a thesis called *The Myth of the Luxuria Stone* by someone named Carl Stork. Plus a shorter professional paper, also by Stork. Both works by Stork were written in 1943. The third folder held a collection of stapled pages, scraps of paper, and articles cut from journals and newspapers.

"Most of the stuff in this folder is relatively recent," I said to Diesel. "Some handwritten notes. A newspaper piece about a museum exhibit that opened last week. An article reprint about Salem witches." I pulled the witch article out and started reading. "Holy cow. This article is about Miriam Lovey being suspected of witchcraft. It says she disappeared before she could be brought to trial. She was fifteen years old at the time."

"Any mention of sexy sonnets?"

"No. But she was accused of inspiring inappropriate desires in men."

Diesel took the article from me and read it for himself. "The whole witch trial thing makes my nuts crawl."

"Boy, I'm really glad you shared that with me."

"Don't you have an equivalent body part that's shriveling even as we speak?"

"No. But I'm getting nauseous."

My doorbell bonged, and someone started pounding. BAM, BAM, BAM! I opened the door and Hatchet charged in, sword drawn.

"Hand it over," he said, "or I will smite thee down."

"You've gotta lose the Renaissance thing," Diesel said to Hatchet. "You sound like an idiot."

"You mock me now, but there will come a time when you will bow to my sire, and to me as well."

Diesel didn't look worried about bowing to Wulf and Hatchet. "There's a reason for this visit, right?"

"You have what is rightly ours. We have the book, and the key is part of the book."

"What key?" Diesel asked.

"You know very well. The Lovey key."

"Nope," Diesel said. "Don't have it."

"You lie. You were in Gilbert Reedy's apartment ahead of me, and you took the key."

"How do you know?" Diesel asked him. "Maybe the police took the key. Maybe the key doesn't exist. Maybe Reedy swallowed the key, and they'll find it during the autopsy."

"I know because I have powers," Hatchet said. "I sense these things. I smell them. I see visions. And besides, I looked in the kitchen window just now, and I saw the key lying on the counter."

"Finders keepers," Diesel said.

Hatchet's eyes almost popped out of their sockets and his face got blotchy. "It will be ours!" he yelled. "My master commands it. You will give me the key or all will die!"

He raised the sword, took a step toward me, and Cat flew through the air and latched onto Hatchet's face.

"YOW!" Hatchet shrieked, dropping his sword, batting at Cat.

Diesel grabbed a handful of Hatchet's

tunic and lifted him off the floor. "I'll take it from here," Diesel said to Cat.

Cat disengaged from Hatchet's face, gracefully landed on the floor, and flicked away a clump of Hatchet's hair that was stuck in his claw.

Diesel carted Hatchet at arm's length to the open door, pitched him out, closed and locked the door.

BAM, BAM, BAM. Hatchet was hammering on the door.

Diesel opened the door and looked down at Hatchet. "Now what?"

Hatchet had a bunch of cat scratches and punctures that were beginning to ooze blood. "I think I left my sword in your living room."

Diesel retrieved the sword, gave it to Hatchet, and closed and locked the door again.

"Have you ever thought about getting shades on those kitchen windows?" Diesel asked me.

"Shades cost money."

"Maybe I should spend the night here. Make sure you're safe."

"Not necessary. I have Cat."

• • •

My clock radio went into music mode at 4:15 A.M. Still dark out. Cat was asleep at the foot of the bed. No rain slashing against the window. All good signs. I dragged myself out of bed, took a shower, and got dressed in my usual uniform of jeans, T-shirt, and sneakers.

The floors throughout the house are wide plank yellow pine. Some very, very old. Some new. The ceilings are low. The walls are old-fashioned plaster. The windows are wood, with small panes. The kitchen is far from high tech, but perfectly functional, and it feels cozy. I have my pots and pans hanging from hooks screwed into ceiling beams over my little work island.

I started coffee brewing, poured some kitty nuggets into a bowl for Cat, and gave him fresh water. I ate a small container of blueberry yogurt while I waited for my coffee, and reviewed my day.

It was Monday. That meant I would make all the usual cupcakes, plus an extra forty-five strawberry for Mr. Nelson's weekly lunch meeting at the boat club. And Clara would need help with the bread, because Mr. Nelson would also want forty-five pretzel rolls. My afternoon and evening were open, but I had a feeling Diesel would fill the empty spaces.

I poured the brewed coffee into a travel mug, added a splash of half-and-half, stuffed myself into a sweatshirt, and grabbed my purse. Diesel had taken the Lovey key and Reedy's papers with him, but the Shakespeare anthology was still on the counter. I stared at the anthology and thought about Hatchet and Wulf . . . that they might be lurking in the dark somewhere between me and my car, waiting to snatch me.

If I'd let Diesel spend the night, he would have protected me against all sorts of drooly, knuckle-dragging, blood-sucking monsters. Problem was, who would protect me from Diesel? Diesel was six foot three inches of mouth-watering, heart-stopping male temptation. He was annoying, charming, pushy, practically leaking testosterone, and he always smelled great. He also was off-limits. According to Diesel, if two people with exceptional abilities do the deed, one of them loses all their special skills, and there's no way to tell which one will lose. It's a total bummer, because if I could be sure it would be me, I'd be happy to make the sacrifice. Unfortunately, if it was Diesel and I had to save the world all by myself, I'd be up the creek without a paddle.

I peeked out the front window at my car. It was sitting under a streetlight only a few steps from my door. No sign of Wulf or Hatchet. Houses were dark across the street. Most of Marblehead was still asleep. Cat was leaning against my leg.

"What do you think?" I asked Cat. "Is it safe?"

Cat blinked, and I took that to mean *yes*.

I opened the door and cautiously stepped outside. I had a plan. If someone came rushing at me, I'd hit him with my purse and kick him in the crotch. I suppose I should also scream, but I hated to wake my neighbors. I locked my door, quickly walked to my car, and jumped behind the wheel. No one came rushing at me. But Wulf appeared out of nowhere, standing motionless, holding my door open, looking down at me.

I couldn't muster enough air to scream, and kicking Wulf in the crotch wasn't an option.

"This isn't a safe place for you," Wulf said, his voice soft and seductive. "And this life you've chosen has limitations. If you played for my team, you would have no limitations. I could give you a new car, your own bakery, a house that doesn't lean downhill." He paused and his eyes softened a little. "I could give you normalcy."

My upper lip broke out in a cold sweat. How did he know I craved normalcy? I reached for the car door and found myself staring at Wulf's perfectly pressed pants. Not a wrinkle in sight. My eyes were at package level, and it was like Baby Bear's bed, not too big and not too small. It looked *just right*.

"Thanks," I said, forcing my attention to move to his eyes. "I'm good."

Thirty minutes later, I rolled into the small lot behind the bakery and parked. Light poured out the open back door of the building and flour floated in the light like fairy dust. Clara was already at work.

Clarinda Dazzle is the latest in a long line of Dazzles who have operated the bakery, stretching back to Puritan times. She owns the historic building, and she lives in a small apartment on the second floor. She's forty years old. She's twice divorced, currently single. She's my height at 5'5", but she seems taller, in part because of her hair. My hair is blond and straight as a pin. Clara's hair is black, shot with gray, possibly shoulder-length, but it's difficult to tell due to the frenzied curls and sheer mass of it all. She's part Wampanoag Indian, but it's a very small part.

I exchanged my sweatshirt for a white chef coat and wrapped a chef apron around my waist.

"It's our usual Monday," Clara said. "Extra pretzel rolls and strawberry cupcakes."

I was already measuring out flour. "I'm on it."

Clara and I don't talk a lot in the morning. Machines whir and hum as bread dough is mechanically kneaded and cake batter is mixed. I move from collecting ingredients to preparing baking pans to shaping yeast dough, my mind focused on the task at hand and the day all bright and shiny in front of me. Usually. Hatchet and Wulf were intruding today. My thoughts kept turning to swords and keys and ugly threats and perfectly pressed pants.

"Are you okay?" Clara asked. "You're talking to yourself, and you're glaring at the sweet roll dough."

"I had a disturbing night. Do you remember Steven Hatchet?"

"Wulf's medieval minion."

"Yeah. I have a key he wants."

"And you don't want to give it to him?"

"No."

"Well, then," Clara said. "Case closed."

CHAPTER FOUR

Glo swung into the kitchen at precisely eight o'clock. She parked her broom in the corner, and set her messenger bag on a shelf.

"The most amazing thing happened last night," she said. "I met this guy online, and he's perfect. I think he's *the one*. And I definitely think he might be a wizard. He didn't come right out and say it, but I got a total vibe."

I looked over at Clara and saw she was working hard to squelch a grimace. Glo was always meeting perfect guys who had the promise of wizardry. I admired her optimism but thought her dating criteria could use some adjustment. None of the guys ever turned out to be a wizard. And some of them were downright scary.

"I'm meeting him for drinks tonight," Glo said. "I have high hopes."

Clara pulled a tray of croissants out of the oven. "The last time you said that, the guy had forty-three piercings and a snake tattooed onto his forehead."

"He was sweet," Glo said. "I'd still be dating him, but he always wanted to wear my clothes, and sometimes he'd wear them home and never return them. I don't mind sharing, but a girl has to draw the line somewhere."

Glo buttoned herself into a blue Dazzle's smock and marched to the front door, where three people were already standing, waiting for the bakery to open. Two hours later, we were between customers, and Glo took the opportunity to box up orders for pickup. Clara was busy scrubbing down her work area, and I was piping frosting onto the last batch of cupcakes. The back door was still open, bringing fresh air and sunshine into the kitchen. A shadow fell across the floor, and we all looked up at Hatchet.

"Let me guess," Clara said. "Sir Hatchet."

"Nay," he said. "Just Hatchet, in service to his lord and master."

"I'm afraid you're in the wrong spot," Clara said. "If you want to buy cupcakes for your lord and master, you need the shop entrance, off the street."

"My liege lord does not require anything so low as a cupcake," Hatchet said. He looked at the tray of newly frosted chocolate cakes, his lips parted, and his eyes glazed over. "Although they doth look tasty."

"Get to the point," I said to Hatchet. "What do you want?"

He snapped to attention. "The key. I will die before I will disappoint my master."

"We could probably arrange that," Clara said.

Hatchet glared at her. "Do not scoff at me. I will have the key. And I will have these cupcakes as well." He grabbed two off the tray and shoved them into his mouth. "Now the key," he said.

Glo had her nose wrinkled. "Dude, you shouldn't talk with your mouth full. Your teeth are all full of chocolate smush."

"The key!" Hatchet said. "I demand that you give me the key!"

"I don't have it," I told him. "Diesel has it."

He drew his sword. "Then I will take you hostage. And I will trade you for the key."

"Hey!" Clara said to Hatchet. "What's wrong with you? You can't go around waving your sword in here. This is a bakery. Have some respect."

"Yeah, and if you don't behave, I'm going to get my broom, and he'll give you a couple good whacks," Glo said.

"Your broom is no match for my sword," Hatchet said. "I'm a skilled swordsman. My aim is deadly true."

"Well, I'm pretty sure my broom might be magic," Glo said.

Hatchet paused for a beat. "How magic?" he asked.

"*Real* magic," Glo said. "About as magic as a broom could get."

Hatchet cut his eyes to me. "I will retreat for now, but I will be back. I will pounce when you least expect it. And I will conjure my own dark powers to battle your evil forces. Stand back now while I take my leave, and thou willst give up these cupcakes."

He stiff-armed his sword in our direction, grabbed the tray of cupcakes, turned, and ran out of the kitchen. A car motor cranked over in the parking lot, and there was the sound of squealing tires on the pavement.

"He needs a pill," Clara said.

Glo shouldered a cookie tray. "I think he's kind of cute. He's just a little misdirected. I might be able to find a spell to help him. I'll have to look in *Ripple's* tonight."

Oh boy, as if Hatchet wasn't crazy enough, now Glo was going to help him.

"What's so special about this key?" Clara asked.

"It's the Lovey key," Glo said. "Remember how I was saving up money so I could buy a book of sonnets, but someone bought it ahead of me? Well, there's a little key that goes with the book, and Carl found it and gave it to Lizzy. And the guy who bought the book, Gilbert Reedy, is dead."

"His death was on the news last night," Clara said. "They said someone broke his neck and threw him off his balcony."

At one o'clock, Diesel showed up. He ambled into the kitchen, slung an arm around my neck, and kissed me on the top of my head.

"What's that about?" I asked him.

"I like you."

"And?"

"I'm hungry."

"For lunch?"

"Yeah, that, too."

"There are some ugly meat pies in the fridge. Sausage, beef with curry, and roasted vegetable."

When a pie or a pastry didn't turn out to be perfect and wonderful, we labeled them ugly and made them available for employee consumption. Diesel grabbed an ugly sausage pie and stood at the counter, eating it cold.

"I haven't read through everything yet," he said, "but a couple interesting things have turned up. Shortly after Reedy got the Lovey book, he joined a dating service. He chose four women from the service because he felt they were looking for true love."

"How do you know?"

"I found a list in the miscellaneous folder. Reedy called them True Love Seekers and sometimes Key Seekers."

"That sounds very adventuresome."

Diesel went back for a second pie. "The list was scribbled on the back of a professional paper written in 1953 promoting the hypothesis that the stones holding the seven deadly sins were originally virtuous. Gluttony represented joy for all things. The bearer of pride had an industrious spirit. . . ."

"And lust?" I asked him.

"Supposedly the Luxuria Stone was originally the stone of true love. The author of the paper theorized that at some point in time, the stone was corrupted and turned sinful. There was an addendum to the paper speculating that a key might exist to find the stone."

"The Lovey key!" Glo said. "I bet Reedy was looking for his true love." She clapped a hand over her heart. "That's so romantic."

"Yeah, and he's so dead," Clara said.

Ten minutes later, I was out of my chef clothes, following Diesel to his car.

"I don't understand why you feel compelled to talk to the four women," I said to him. "It's not like Reedy was in a relationship with any of them. How could this possibly help you find the stone?"

"It's a place to start," Diesel said. "I've got home addresses and work addresses for all of them. Cassandra McGinty is the first on the list. She lives in Lynn, and she waits tables at a restaurant in Salem. I called the restaurant, and they said she doesn't come in until four, so I thought we'd see if she's home."

Lynn is on the North Shore, south of Marblehead. It's a diverse seaside town with a sketchy history and a hardworking population. Cassandra McGinty lived in a big clapboard house on the west side of Lynn. The house had been converted to apartments, and Cassandra's was on the third floor.

I huffed and puffed up the stairs and stood back while Diesel knocked on the door. A woman with enormous breasts and short, punked-up white blond hair answered. She was early twenties, medium height, and slim except for her chest. She was wearing spike heels, tight jeans, and a spaghetti-strap tank top that showed a quarter mile of cleavage.

Diesel checked out the breasts and smiled, his eyes locked in at nipple level. "I'm looking for Cassandra McGinty."

"Well, you've found her," McGinty said, looking Diesel up and down.

I wanted to kick Diesel in the back of his leg to see if I could knock his eyes loose, but I'd kicked him yesterday and didn't want it to become habit-forming. So I stepped around him and extended my hand.

"I'm Lizzy Tucker," I said. "The stupid drooling guy is Diesel. We'd like to talk to you about Gilbert Reedy."

"Are you cops?" she asked. "I heard Gilbert tried to fly off his balcony and it didn't turn out so good."

"Were you dating him?" I asked her.

"Gilbert and I met for coffee, but that was all. I don't know if you saw Gilbert before he turned himself into a pancake on the sidewalk, but he wasn't exactly hot." She did another full body scan of Diesel. "And I like hot men."

"Gee, too bad I don't know any or I'd bring them around," I said to McGinty. "Diesel here looks good, but he bats for the other team, if you know what I mean."

"Lucky them," McGinty said.

"We're looking for a book of sonnets. It was missing from Reedy's apartment."

"He had a book with him when we had coffee. It was real old looking, and he read this lame poem to me from it. Something about a hot eye."

"Do you remember anything else about the poem?"

"Yeah. I remember wanting it to end. Gilbert Reedy was the king of geeks."

"He was looking for his true love," I told her.

"Me, too," McGinty said. "But I want one with a big package."

We thanked McGinty for her help, trucked down the stairs, and got back into Diesel's SUV.

"I might have been her true love if you hadn't ruined it with that fib," Diesel said. "I have all the requirements."

"You were looking at her like she was a free pass to the Super Bowl. I was afraid you were going to step on your tongue."

CHAPTER FIVE

Gail Danko was second on the list. She lived in a small, bedraggled bungalow a half mile from Cassandra McGinty. A black Sentra was parked in the driveway. It was showing some rust and a few good-size dents. A gray cat sat on the roof, enjoying the afternoon sun.

"Danko is a nurse, but she's off on sick leave," Diesel said. "Divorced. No kids."

He knocked on the door, the door opened, and a short, round woman with a big fluffy white cat under her arm and her foot in a cast looked out at us. "What?"

"I'm looking for Gail Danko," Diesel said.

The woman's eyes glazed over for a moment while she took Diesel in. "Mm-mmm," she said.

Diesel smiled at her. "Why is your cat wearing pants?"

"She's a national champion, and she's in heat. We're going to breed her tomorrow."

The cat on the car gave a loud *YOWL* and the national champion jumped out of Danko's arms and shot out the door.

"Miss Snowball!" Danko shouted. "Help! Catch her! She can't get pregnant from that alley cat!"

In a flash, Snowball was out of sight, running as fast as she could in her cat diaper, the gray cat close on her tail. Gail Danko stomped onto her little porch with her plaster-coated foot and single crutch, but she clearly wasn't going to catch Snowball.

"Don't worry," I said to Danko. "Diesel will track Miss Snowball down. He's good at this. He has special tracking skills."

"I don't track cats," Diesel said.

"Of course you do," I told him. "You have that whole energy sensitivity thing. That's why you're the bounty hunter."

"I can find *people*."

"Are you sure you can't find cats? Have you ever tried to sniff one out?"

"No," Diesel said, "but Miss Whatever shouldn't be hard to find. Speaking from the male perspective, they're probably just around the corner in the bushes, trying to get her pants off."

He disappeared around the side of the building, and Danko and I stood waiting.

"What happened to your foot?" I asked her.

"Bunion surgery," she said. "I've been sitting with the stupid thing elevated for two weeks, doing nothing but eating. I was struggling with my weight before the surgery, and now I'm totally *fat*. And if that isn't bad enough, Miss Snowball's going to get pregnant with that trailer-trash tomcat." There was some god-awful screeching and howling, and Danko stumbled back and put her hand to her heart. "My baby!"

"It might not be so bad," I said. "She could be faking it. I mean, who hasn't faked it once or twice, right?"

A moment later, Diesel emerged from behind the house with Miss Snowball. The diaper was shredded but still attached, her fur was standing straight out, and her eyes were almost popped out of their sockets.

"Was that you screeching and howling?" I asked Diesel.

"Princess wasn't happy with hotshot's foreplay technique." He handed Snowball over to Danko. "I hope the cat you've got coming tomorrow knows what he's doing."

"We wanted to ask you about Gilbert Reedy," I said to Danko. "I believe you dated."

"We met for coffee, but he started wheezing after five minutes. Turns out he's allergic to cats."

"Did he say anything interesting in those five minutes?" I asked her. "Did he mention a key?"

"No. He said on his form that he had

the key to finding true love, but that was it. Hard to talk about keys and true love when you're having an asthma attack."

Diesel backtracked to Salem and parked in the lot of the public library. "Sharon Gordon is third on the list. She's a librarian. Thirty-six years old. She lives with her mother. And her Facebook page says she likes Nora Roberts, s'mores, and penguins."

"You can trust a woman who likes s'mores," I said. "It's the gooey factor."

"Something to keep in mind."

We entered the building and found Gordon shelving books in the children's section. She was tall and slim, with brown hair pulled back in a clip at the nape of her neck. She was wearing a pale pink knit top, tan slacks, and flats.

She gasped when she turned and saw Diesel. "Sorry," she said. "I'm used to seeing short people in this room."

"We'd like to talk to you about Gilbert Reedy," Diesel said.

"Are you police?"

Diesel picked a picture book about

trucks off her cart and paged through it. "That's a complicated question."

Sharon pushed her cart forward and placed a book on a shelf. "I met Gilbert through a dating service. He said he was looking for true love."

"And?"

She shrugged. "We went out a couple times, and I thought he liked me, and then this woman named Ann came along, and he got weird and dumped me."

"Do you have a last name for her?"

"No. I don't know anything about her." She shelved another book. "I'll tell you one thing, though—Gilbert Reedy was a very strange man. His area of expertise was Elizabethan England, but he was obsessed with an obscure poet from the nineteenth century. He had a little book of sonnets he could quote by heart. He was convinced it held the key to true love. Like it had mystical powers. And then one day last week, he called me up and said he didn't need me anymore. That was the way he put it. He didn't *need* me. Can you imagine? How am I supposed to interpret that? And he was babbling about Ann, Ann, Ann. And good triumphing over evil. And he should have seen it sooner."

"What should he have seen sooner?" I asked her.

"He didn't say. He was on a rant, making no sense. If it was anyone else, I'd think they were on drugs, but Gilbert Reedy wouldn't have any idea where to *get* drugs. He was a total academic. It was almost like dating me was a science experiment."

"Did he carry the book of sonnets with him?" Diesel asked. "Did you see it?"

"Yes. It was actually very wonderful. The sonnets were written by a man named Lovey, and the book cover was leather with hand-tooled almond blossoms scrawled across it. It reminded me of the Van Gogh painting. I did a little of my own research and found that Van Gogh and Lovey were contemporaries, so it's possible Lovey copied the painting to decorate his book. Or it could just have been coincidence. The almond blossom has long been a symbol of hope. The book locked like a diary, and there was a little key that went with the book, but Gilbert never let me see the key. He said it was the last piece to the puzzle, and he kept it someplace *safe*."

"What did he mean by the last piece to the puzzle?" I asked her.

"I don't know," Gordon said. "He was always making statements like that and then jumping off to something else. In retrospect, I'm not sure why I kept going out with him. He was sort of a crackpot."

"He read poetry to you, and he was searching for true love," I said.

Gordon smiled and nodded. "Yes. He was a *romantic* crackpot."

"Do you have any idea who might know something about the key and the puzzle?" I asked her. "Did he have any close relatives or friends that he might have spoken to?"

"I don't think he had friends, and he didn't talk about his relatives. He mentioned his grad student a lot. Julie. He was her thesis advisor. He thought she was smart. He might have confided in her. And of course there's Ann."

We left the library and returned to the SUV.

"You said Reedy had chosen four women from the dating service," I said to Diesel. "Is Ann the fourth?"

"No. Deirdre Early is the fourth. She has a Boston address."

I looked at my watch. "It's almost four o'clock. Do you want to keep going with this?"

"Yeah. I'd like to poke around Harvard and see if I can find Reedy's grad student. And then we can try to catch Early on our way home."

Diesel tapped a number into his cell phone and asked for assistance in contacting Reedy's grad student. "I'll be in Cambridge in an hour," he said. "See if you can get her to meet me. And I'd like to see Reedy's office."

"Was that your assistant?" I asked him when he disconnected.

"More or less."

Diesel's been through six assistants in the short time I've known him. I've stopped trying to remember names.

They never have faces. They're always just voices floating out of the hands-free car phone, brought to Diesel through the miracle of Bluetooth.

We took 1A to Boston. The landscape was interesting at first and then turned ugly with potholed highways and crazy angry drivers careening around insane traffic circles that shot roads off in all directions.

We left the North Shore and connected to Storrow Drive, rolling through Boston, following the Charles River. The back sides of four-story redbrick town houses hugged the left side of the road, with Boston's high-rise office and condo buildings rising beyond them. I knew that tree-lined streets of prime real estate row houses ran for a couple blocks in from Storrow, ending with the two high-end boutique shopping streets, Newbury and Boylston. The Public Garden was at one end of Newbury, and the large indoor shopping mall was at the other end. And if you walked far enough south, you came to Fenway Park, home of the Red Sox.

A narrow patch of grass and a bike

path stretched along the river side of Storrow. A few people pedaled along the bike path, and a few hardy souls were out on the river in small sailboats. We passed an empty bandshell and some Porta-Potties left from a weekend event.

Diesel drove the length of Storrow and took the bridge over the Charles River to Cambridge. I was in foreign territory now. I'd made lots of trips to downtown Boston since moving to Marblehead, but I've never ventured across the river to Cambridge.

"You look like you know where you're going," I said to Diesel.

"I spent some time here two years ago, looking for someone."

"Did you find him?"

"Yeah."

"And?"

Diesel stopped for a light. "It's complicated."

"You didn't kill him, did you?"

"I don't kill people."

"Did you turn him into a toad?"

Diesel glanced over at me and smiled. I wasn't sure what the smile meant, and I wasn't sure I wanted to know, so I stared out the window at the passing buildings and sidewalks filled with college students. "Did we just pass Harvard?" I asked him.

"No," Diesel said. "That was MIT. Harvard is a couple miles up Massachusetts Avenue."

Mass Ave was four-lanes wide, and traffic was heavy but moving. Buildings were a mix of more high-rise offices and condos, plus lower-profile furniture stores, ethnic restaurants, bakeries, bike stores, car dealerships, churches, bookshops, and hotels.

Diesel's phone rang and a woman's voice came up. "Julie Brodsky will meet you in the front lobby of the Barker Center, 12 Quincy Street. Follow Mass Ave to Harvard Yard and bear right after you pass the Inn. The building is on the corner of Quincy and Harvard streets. I told her you were Daniel Crowley, Reedy's cousin from Chicago."

"Nice," Diesel said. "Thanks." And he hung up.

"Where does your assistant live?" I asked him.

"Don't know."

"Have you seen this one?"

"Nope."

"You go through a lot of assistants."

"So I've been told."

"Why do you suppose that is?" I asked him.

"I've heard rumors that I'm considered high maintenance with low reward."

"Imagine that."

"Listen, when I'm hunting someone down in the Thar Desert in India, I've got dysentery, and my camel runs away, I expect a new camel to show up *fast*."

"Seems like a reasonable request. How often does that happen?"

"More often than I'd care to remember."

CHAPTER SIX

Diesel drove past the Inn, turned right, and cruised around until he found on-street parking. Sidewalks and buildings were redbrick, there were a lot of grassy spaces, and I had the feeling I was in a small town inside a city. It was sunny, but there was a chill to the air, and people were wearing sweatshirts and sweaters and had long knit scarves wrapped around their necks.

We entered the courtyard to Barker Center from Quincy Street and had no trouble locating Reedy's grad student. She was wearing jeans and a bulky, tweedy sweater, and she was hugging a copy of *The History of English Sixteenth-Century Verse*. She had brown, super-curly hair pulled back into a ponytail that was a big round puffball. No makeup. Large, round, red-framed glasses. Five feet, two inches tall. First impression was that she was twelve years old. On closer inspection, there were a few faint laugh lines around her eyes.

Diesel introduced himself as Daniel Crowley, and Julie's eyes filled with tears.

"I'm so sorry for your loss," she said. "Dr. Reedy was a wonderful man."

"I was hoping to see his office," Diesel said. "I gave him a book several years ago that has sentimental value. I'd like it back, and it wasn't in his condo."

"Of course. I can take you to his office. The police have already been here, but they didn't take anything. They looked around, rolled their eyes, and left. We've been waiting for his family to clean things out, but so far you're the only one who's come forward."

We followed her one flight up, down the hall, and stopped at the doorway to

Reedy's office. It was instantly clear why the police rolled their eyes and left. The office was clogged with assorted professorial flotsam. Books overflowed the bookshelves and were stacked everywhere. Artifacts were stuck away in nooks and crannies. Rolled-up maps were scattered on the floor and desktop.

"Wow," I said. "There's a lot of stuff here. His condo was so neat. It's like he was two different people."

"He slept in his condo, but he lived here," Julie said. "For that matter, I know there were nights when he worked late and slept here. There's a couch buried under all those books and tapestries. His area of expertise was Elizabethan literature, but his passion was a forgotten poet of the late 1800s, John Lovey. Dr. Reedy stumbled upon some of Lovey's sonnets ten years ago and was deeply affected by them. I think at heart Dr. Reedy was a true romantic."

"Have you read the sonnets?" I asked her.

"Yes, but I have to admit I wasn't as taken with them as Dr. Reedy." She went to the desk and shuffled through some papers. "He wrote a scholarly paper on Lovey's work and life. I know there's a copy here somewhere. It's very interesting. It seems that during Lovey's time he was regarded as a visionary philosopher. Sort of an Ayn Rand. He had a small but dedicated cult following. They were all devoted to the search for true love." She moved to a different stack of papers and began picking her way through it. "Lovey's most ardent follower was a man named Abner Goodfellow. He lived in Hanover, New Hampshire, and Abner's house is still in the Goodfellow family. Dr. Reedy visited Abner's great-great-great-granddaughter, and she allowed him to prowl through the attic, which was filled to the rafters with all sorts of ancient treasures. At least Dr. Reedy said they were treasures, but I suspect much of it was the usual junk that collects over time in attics and garages." She pulled some pages out of the pile and waved them in the air. "I found it!"

Diesel took the paper from her. "Can I keep this?"

"Of course." She looked around the room. "Dr. Reedy was so absorbed in his work for the last couple months I'm afraid this office has gotten even messier than usual. Maybe I can help you find your book. What did it look like?"

"It was a signed copy of *The Wind in the Willows,*" Diesel said. "Gilbert loved Mr. Toad."

"I don't remember ever seeing it," Julie said, "but I'll look on this side of the room, and you look through the bookcase."

I went to his desk and systematically went through the drawers. The top right-side drawer was locked with no key in sight, so I got Diesel to do his magical unlocking thing. He opened the drawer, and we stared at a leather-bound book that I suspected might be similar to the book of sonnets. Hand-tooled cover and a small locking clasp. In this case, the cover design was an elaborate *A* and *G*.

"It's Abner's diary," Julie said, looking across the desk. "Dr. Reedy stumbled onto it when he was in Abner's attic. Among other things, it describes the final days of Lovey's life and details what

Lovey told Abner Goodfellow moments before Lovey's death. Dr. Reedy took it as gospel, but I thought it sounded like a very sick old man returning to a favorite childhood fairy tale." Julie did a fast scan of the room. "I'm not sure you're going to find your book here. Maybe you'd like to take the diary in its place. It was one of Dr. Reedy's most prized possessions. I believe the little key is in the drawer with the diary."

"I'd love to have the diary," Diesel said, taking the diary and the key. "That's very generous of you. I appreciate all your help."

"Perhaps you could locate the rest of his family and let them know he has some wonderful things here."

"For sure," Diesel said. "Thanks again."

Deirdre Early lived on Commonwealth Avenue in the Back Bay section of Boston. It was a short distance from Harvard, but it had taken us over an hour in rush-hour traffic that included a car fire on the Harry Houdini bridge. Fortunately, the car had pretty much burned itself out by the time we reached the bridge, and traffic was moving. Diesel circled Early's block once looking for a parking place. When he returned to her address the second time, there was a car missing, and he pulled in.

"How do you always manage to get a parking place?" I asked him, halfway afraid that some unsuspecting car had gotten beamed up into space by an unknown entity.

"Positive thinking," Diesel said. "And I'm exceptionally lucky . . . usually."

"Usually?"

"There's been the occasional lapse."

Early's narrow, three-story row house had a postage-stamp front yard that might have been amazing in the summer, but at present time was a tangle of dead vines and shriveled shrubs. The façade was dark gray stone. The roof was gray slate. There were drapes on the windows with no light shining through. The door and wood trim were black.

"Holy cats," I said to Diesel, taking the house in.

"Grim," Diesel said.

We walked to the front door, rang the

bell, and a woman answered. She was movie star beautiful, with glossy midnight black hair cut into a short bob. She had long black lashes, and she was wearing bright red lip gloss. She was my height but much more voluptuous in a silky low-cut black shirt, tight black pencil skirt, and four-inch spike-heeled pumps.

"Deirdre Early?" Diesel asked.

"Yes," she said. "And you?"

"Diesel."

Her smile was small and didn't reach her eyes. "Interesting," she said.

Diesel didn't return the smile. "I'd like to talk to you about Gilbert Reedy."

"Poor man," she said. "Would you like to come in?"

We stepped into her foyer and stopped there. I could see her living room and dining room from where I was standing. Very formal. Oriental rugs. Fabrics were burgundy and gold. Dark woods. Crystal chandelier over the table.

"I believe you dated Reedy," Diesel said.

She crossed her arms over her chest. "Briefly. He's dead, you know."

"You have a lovely home," I said to her.

She flicked her eyes to me. "Thank you. I don't believe we've met."

"Lizzy Tucker."

She studied me for a moment and turned back to Diesel. "Your move," she said to him.

"Were you looking for true love?" Diesel asked her.

"Of course. Isn't that everyone's goal? Do you want true love?"

"Not at the moment," Diesel said.

She looked at him from under lowered lashes. "Pity."

"And what about nineteenth-century poets?" Diesel asked Early. "Are you fond of them?"

"With a passion. And you?"

"Not so much."

"Hmm. I thought we would've had more in common," Early said. "If you'll excuse me now, I have a dinner engagement."

We left Back Bay, and we didn't speak until we were on the 1A, heading home.

"That was weird," I said to Diesel. "The house was pretty inside but oppressive. And I had the feeling you knew each other."

"We've never met, but it's possible she's heard of me. And the negative energy you felt was from her. It was rolling off her in waves. If I stayed there much longer, I would have started bleeding from my ears."

"Omigod. Would you really bleed from your ears?"

Diesel grinned at me. "No. I was exaggerating."

"Deirdre Early isn't normal."

"Not even a little," Diesel said.

"I suppose we aren't normal, either."

"The only normal people are people you don't know very well."

"That's a quote from a famous person," I told him.

"Yeah. I think it was either Andy Griffith or Yoda."

CHAPTER SEVEN

Diesel took me back to my car and I went straight home. I made a grilled cheese for dinner, cleaned the kitchen, and threw some laundry in the washer. I surfed through a bunch of channels on television and gave up. Diesel was in his apartment reading the Goodfellow diary, and I was finding that while I'd wished for a quiet night to myself, it wasn't working. I couldn't get my mind off Gilbert Reedy, Deirdre Early, Lovey, and the Luxuria Stone. It was all in a mix in my head, going round and round. I called

Glo and asked how late the Exotica Shoppe stayed open.

"Usually until nine o'clock," Glo said. "Sometimes later in October because of Halloween. I could go with you if you're thinking of shopping."

"Don't you have a date tonight?"

"No. He called to say he was being detained, and I didn't have enough money to bail him out. I never bail someone out on the first date anymore. Been there, done that."

Thirty minutes later, I had Glo and her broom in my car, and we were headed for the Exotica Shoppe.

"This is way exciting," Glo said. "I wanted the sonnets because they were hot, but this is better. They're like magical and mystical. And I'm really into this whole saving mankind from descending into hell. I mean, it's one thing to go green, but rescuing mankind from Satan is *big*."

Ye Olde Exotica Shoppe is located two blocks south of Dazzle's Bakery. The name is written in gold script above the ancient wood door. The sign in the window reads OPEN and dares people to come inside. Exotica gets a lot of tourist trade, but believers in the occult and history buffs shop there as well. It's a small store stocked floor to ceiling with who-knows-what. Jars are labeled for self-serve convenience. Pig ears, troll phlegm, dried dragon tongue, screech owl beaks, Gummi Bears, milkweed pods, bullock tails, kosher salt, Irish pixie dust, candied earthworm, rotted beetle brain, Belgian white rabbit gonads, and much, much more.

Nina Wortley is the owner-manager of Exotica. She's in her early sixties. She has long, frizzed, snow-white hair. Her face looks like it's been dusted with cake flour, and her bony fingers are loaded with all sorts of rings. She favors floor-length, silky, midnight blue capes and frothy white gowns that she gets from the overstock costume store two doors down. And she accessorizes this fantasy fashion ensemble with sensible wool socks and Birkenstock clogs.

Nina smiled when she saw Glo. "I was just thinking about you. I got in a new shipment of powdered orange spotted toad. I believe Ripple called for a smidgen in his recipe for controlling barking in enchanted objects."

"Thanks," Glo said, "but I don't have a barking problem."

Nina cut her eyes to Glo's broom. "Has his mood improved with the extract of contented cow?"

"Maybe a little."

"Well, if he starts barking, I have just the thing."

After five minutes in the Exotica Shoppe with Glo and Nina, *I* was ready to start barking. Bad enough I had to deal with Diesel and the whole *abilities beyond normal* thing. Glo and Nina took suspension of disbelief to a whole other level.

"I want to talk to you about the Lovey book of sonnets," I said to Nina.

"You're the third person to ask about it since the professor was killed," Nina said.

"We want to know everything," Glo said. "We're investigating, and we might save mankind from Armageddon."

"That would be excellent," Nina said. "Let me know if you need help. I have a few spells I've been saving for a special occasion . . . like doomsday."

"Was Gilbert Reedy a regular customer?" I asked Nina.

"No. He happened to walk past the shop and saw the book in the window. He was very excited about it. He knew the entire history. He said it completed his collection."

"Who else came in and asked about the book?"

"A vampire. He was supernaturally handsome. He had shoulder-length black hair, and deathly pale skin. He came in the same day the professor was killed. He wanted to know if the key had been sold with the book. And then a woman came in a day later and asked the very same question."

"Do you know the woman's name?"

"No. She was waiting outside for me to open the store. She was pacing and smoking. And her hair was every which way, as if she'd been running her hands through it."

"Short black hair?" I asked.

"Yes."

"My age?"

"Maybe a little older."

"Pretty?"

"Beastly. She was practically snarling. She said I was ten minutes late. And she *demanded* I tell her the location of the little key. Can you imagine?"

"Did you tell her?"

"I told her it was sold with the book. And then I offered her a Zuzu wafer because she was so angry and I thought it would calm her. They're very delicate and they smell wonderful. Like cinnamon and roses. They're made from shortbread dough rolled paper thin and infused with essence of crushed Zuzu berries."

"And these cookies make you happy?" Glo asked.

"No," Nina said. "They give you diarrhea. Zuzu is really nasty stuff."

"Has anyone else asked about the book or the key?" I asked Nina.

"That's it so far."

"Do you have any other books by Lovey?"

"No. I just had the one. I don't even know when I acquired it. I was dusting one of the top shelves, and I came across it and was taken with the engraved cover. Anyway, I put it in the window and did a little research on it."

"I bet you used Ryan's *Big Book of Enchanted Works,*" Glo said.

Nina straightened a row of glass jars holding pickled eyeballs. "Actually, I Googled it. You know, the Internet. There wasn't a lot out there . . . just that his sonnets were said to inspire lust and some woman was accused of witchery because of them. I don't think she was ever convicted."

We left Nina, and we went to a nearby pub. Glo and I got cheeseburgers and beer. Broom didn't seem to want anything.

"He never eats when people are watching," Glo said.

"He's a broom," I said to Glo. "Brooms don't eat."

"True, but I'm pretty sure he's an enchanted broom. And sometimes when I get up in the morning, food is missing. Once there was a half-eaten bagel on my kitchen counter, and I know I didn't eat it."

I looked at Broom, leaning nonchalantly in the corner, against the back of the booth, and I thought he might have twitched a little. Probably, he was laughing at us.

"Too bad about your date tonight," I said to Glo. "Why was he arrested?"

"The usual. He shot someone in the head with a nail gun. Honestly, I'm going to stop going out with carpenters. This is getting really old."

It was after ten when I got home, and Cat was waiting for me. I closed and locked the door and bent to scratch Cat behind his ear. We went into the kitchen, I gave him a pumpkin muffin and some milk, and waited while he ate.

"I had another one of those strange days," I said to Cat. "Diesel thinks the hunt is on for one of the SALIGIA Stones, and it looks like someone was killed because of it. What do you think?"

Cat looked up at me and blinked.

"Yeah," I said. "That's what I think, too."

I turned the lights off, and Cat and I padded up the stairs to my bedroom.

My bedroom walls are pale green, and the sheers on the window are white and floaty. I found my bed in a secondhand store, and it was exactly what I wanted. It's queen-size and has a wrought-iron frame that has a fanciful, scrolly design on the headboard and footboard. I have a small table and lamp at bedside, and a small chest of drawers at the foot of the bed. No television. Just a notepad and pen on the table, and a book.

I puffed my pillows and snuggled under my genuine synthetic down comforter. Cat curled at my feet.

"This is the good life," I said to Cat.

Cat didn't look around at me. Cat knew it was good. Probably, he would think it was even better if he hadn't been neutered, but there wasn't much I could do about that. I thought about reading a few pages, but that's as far as it went. It had been a long day, my stomach was full of cheeseburger, and I was tired.

I never have problems falling asleep, and I rarely wake up in the middle of the night. My eyes open every morning at 4:10 A.M., which is five minutes before my alarm goes off. So it was odd to wake to a dark room and see 2:00 on the digital display of my clock radio. I lay very still, barely breathing, listening, knowing something had dragged me out of sleep. My eyes adjusted to the dark, and I saw that Cat was crouched in the middle of the bed, his tail bristled out like a bottle brush, his attention riveted on a shadow at the far end of the room. I realized the shadow was a man, and my heart stopped for a moment.

It was Wulf. He was standing statue-still, silently watching me.

"How long have you been here?" I asked him, my voice barely above a whisper.

"Not long."

"What do you want?"

"Compliance. I want you to stop helping my foolish cousin. Without you, he would be forced to give up and move on."

"I can't see him doing that."

"He would have no choice. He would be ineffective."

"Why do you want him to give up?"

"I have my reasons. And some of the answer is obvious. I need to secure the

Luxuria Stone, and he's making it more difficult than it should be."

"I'll think about it," I told him.

Truth is I'd tell him *anything* if I thought it would get him out of my bedroom.

"You have no idea how dangerous this hunt is," Wulf said. "This isn't a game. There will be terrible consequences if you continue."

There was a flash of light, Cat growled low in his throat, and when the smoke cleared, Wulf was gone. I didn't hear him leave. No footsteps on my stairs. I didn't hear a door open or close. Only the rumble of an expensive car engine catching on the street below my window.

"Jeez Louise," I said to Cat.

I switched my bedside light on and debated calling Diesel. It would be comforting, but it wouldn't really serve a purpose. Wulf was gone. At least for now. I got up and turned every light in the house on, and checked to make sure all the doors were locked. I grabbed some cloves of garlic and my big chef knife, and I went back to bed. Okay, I know garlic is for vampires, and I don't think I believe in vampires. At least I don't *want* to believe in vampires. And Wulf probably isn't a vampire. Still, it can't hurt to carry some garlic with me just in case, right?

CHAPTER EIGHT

Clara watched me pipe frosting onto a batch of spice cupcakes. “You look like you’re asleep on your feet,” she said. “You just frosted a cupcake with your eyes closed.”

“I had a bad night. Wulf popped into my bedroom at two in the morning, and I couldn’t get back to sleep after he left.”

“He *popped* in?”

“I woke up and there he was . . . watching me.”

“That’s creepy. What did he want? Did he attack you?”

“No. He wanted to talk. The conversation ran somewhere between a threat and a warning. He wanted me to stop helping Diesel."

"Maybe that's not such a bad idea," Clara said.

Glo had been listening from the doorway. "She can't stop helping Diesel. She has to save the world or we'll all go to hell."

"Hell would be a bummer," Clara said.

Personally, I thought we were in big trouble if I was the one standing between the world's population and hell.

"I need coffee," I said to Clara. "I need a nap."

I left work early, drove home, and crashed into bed. When I woke up, Diesel was standing, hands on hips, looking down at me.

"Could you ring a doorbell?" I said to him. "I'm tired of men barging into my house. Whatever happened to privacy?"

"Is someone barging in besides me?"

"Wulf. He dropped in last night to tell me I should stop helping you or else."

"Or else what?"

"He didn't say, but I don't think it was good. Big trouble. Lots of danger. That sort of thing. He said if I stopped helping you, you'd go away."

"I wouldn't go away," Diesel said, "but I'd be severely limited. He'd have a huge advantage."

I sat up and swung my legs over the side of the bed. "Did you read Goodfellow's diary?"

"Yeah, and it wasn't easy. Almost a hundred pages written in cramped script, detailing everything from the purchase of chickens to indigestion. And he had indigestion *a lot*."

"What did he say about Lovey?"

"Lovey told Goodfellow he was in possession of an ancient artifact, a stone of great and terrible power, and it was a horrible burden that he wasn't able to shed. He couldn't destroy the stone, and he couldn't part with it. When the stone was passed to Lovey by a distant relative, he was warned of the damage the stone could do if its evil energy was ever released. He was also told that the stone wasn't always evil. The stone that now brought people to their knees with lust . . ."

I did an inadvertent giggle.

Diesel grinned down at me. "Lizzy Tucker, you have a dirty mind."

"Sorry."

"I like it. It shows potential."

"Get back to Goodfellow."

"Lovey told Goodfellow the stone was originally pure. It originally held the power of true love, but it had been corrupted by an evil force, just as all the Stones of SALIGIA had been corrupted long ago. Lovey was convinced the stone could be restored to its original purity, and that it could bring true love to him and to the world. Unfortunately, Lovey never found out how to remove the curse on the stone. Sensing his life was about to end, he hid the stone for safekeeping, leaving behind cleverly disguised clues. Goodfellow writes that only a believer in true love will have the ability to find the clues and the stone."

"What do you think?"

Diesel shrugged. "It doesn't matter what I think. My job is to keep the stones out of Wulf's hands. For what it's worth, when I read the paper I got off Reedy's desk, the one written in 1953, it was the first time I heard this version. For centuries, people have searched for the stones. The possibility that the stones could be uncorrupted is new to me."

"It's a nice thought."

"I guess, but I don't want to go down in history books as the guy who rid the world of lust. Speaking for myself, I like lust a lot. And to be honest, the whole true love thing feels kinda girly to me."

"I must be getting used to you," I said. "I'm only a little horrified."

Diesel grinned. "It's all about lowered expectations." He stretched, and scratched his stomach. "I'm hungry. Do you have any more pumpkin muffins left?"

I shoved my feet into my sneakers and laced them up. "I have pumpkin muffins and blueberry muffins. And I think you're an idiot."

"Yeah, I get that a lot."

Diesel followed me down the stairs and chose a blueberry muffin. "I'd like to go back to Harvard," he said. "I have some questions for Julie. I don't get the dating thing. At first I thought Reedy believed the sonnets would bring him true love somehow, and all he had to do was find the right woman, but that's not it. The women were part of the search for the stone. I don't think Reedy was interested in finding his own true love."

An hour later, we met Julie in Reedy's office.

"Unfortunately, I only have a few minutes," Julie said. "I have a class at the top of the hour."

"I appreciate the few minutes," Diesel said. "Some women have come forward saying they dated Dr. Reedy recently. The family would like to know if he was serious about any of these women. We thought you might know."

"First, let me say that I had the utmost respect for Dr. Reedy. And in fact I believe he considered me to be a good friend. Putting all this aside, I have to tell you he wasn't always the most rational of men when it came to anything connected to John Lovey. He believed the Lovey sonnet book was a huge breakthrough. He said it contained the first clue to the Luxuria Stone's location. He even paid a visit to someone in Louisburg Square who, according to Dr.

Reedy, owned the object that held the next clue."

"Do you know what the object or the next clue was?" Diesel asked.

"No. Only that Dr. Reedy got to see the object that held the clue, but he couldn't decipher it. His contention was that only someone who believed in true love could decipher the clue. Call me a cynic, but I think it's possible there simply wasn't a clue."

"So he was looking for a woman who believed in true love to decipher the second clue," I said to Julie.

She nodded and checked her watch. "Yes. I'm sorry, but I'm afraid I have to run."

"One final question," Diesel said. "Who was Ann?"

Some color rose to Julie's cheeks. "She was another one of the true-love women. The last, so far as I know. And Dr. Reedy changed after meeting her. He became agitated and untrusting. He even accused me of spying on him when I was waiting outside his office for our weekly meeting."

"Do you know anything about her? Last name? What she looked like?"

"No. Nothing. Only Ann."

Julie left, but we stayed in Reedy's office.

"There has to be something here to help us," Diesel said. "A Beacon Hill address on a scrap of paper. A map. A phone number for Ann."

"I imagine it would help if we had the book of sonnets."

"Only if we knew what we were looking for. Wulf has the book, but I don't see him moving forward. He's got Hatchet trying to steal the key. My guess is he needs the key for something more than just opening the book. I'm sure Wulf has already opened the book without the key."

I sat in Reedy's chair and studied his desktop. I'd already gone through everything on his desk and in his drawers the other day, but I repeated my search. It seemed to me that if a clue existed, it would be close at hand. Reedy would have been at his desk, taking notes, doing his research. One of the items on his desk was a book on the life and works of Vincent van Gogh. It hadn't seemed significant yesterday, but today it caught my attention because I remembered the librarian saying the cover on Lovey's book of sonnets reminded her of Van Gogh's almond blossom painting. I thumbed through the book and found the painting. Oil on canvas. Branches and blossoms against a blue sky. Completed in 1890. It was owned by the Van Gogh Museum in Amsterdam, but it was currently part of a traveling exhibit.

The page was held by a computer printout of what at first glance appeared to be the same painting, but on closer inspection showed small differences. Someone had circled the differences and written *private collection* and a Louisburg Square address in the margin.

"I think I might have something," I said to Diesel. "Come look at this. The librarian said the Lovey book cover reminded her of a Van Gogh painting of almond blossoms. I found this art book on Reedy's desk, and it looks like there were two almond blossom paintings that were similar but different. One is owned by a museum, but it looks like the second is in a private collection. There's a Louisburg Square address here, and Julie said Reedy went to see someone in Louisburg Square about the clue."

Diesel looked over my shoulder and ruffled my hair. "Way to go, Sherlock."

Beacon Hill is a Boston neighborhood delineated by the Boston Common, the Charles River, and busy Cambridge Street. Streets are narrow, lit by gaslight, and mostly one way. No matter where you want to go on Beacon Hill, if you're driving, you can't get there from wherever you happen to be. Sidewalks are uneven from time and tree roots. Residences are primarily Federalist-style town houses, with some Greek Revival thrown in for variety. Charles Street slices through the residential area from one end to the other, with its antiques shops, restaurants, boutique stores, coffee shops, bakeries, and greengrocers. Louisburg Square sits two blocks uphill from Charles. The Square itself is a green oasis surrounded by a black wrought-iron fence and a sprinkling of trees. Houses around the Square are redbrick with black shutters, and usually five floors, with half of one floor belowground, opening out to a tiny backyard. This is high-end Boston real estate, with houses selling for multimillions of dollars. I'd walked the streets as a tourist, from Charles Street, up Beacon, to the Massachusetts State House, so I had a vague understanding of the geography.

Diesel left Storrow Drive for the flat of the hill, found Mt. Vernon Street, and turned into Louisburg Square. He counted off houses and idled in front of a perfectly renovated town house that sat in the middle of the block.

"This is the address on the computer printout," he said. "According to the text I just got from my assistant, the house is owned by Gerald Belker. He's president of Belker Extrusion. Has a wife and two adult children. This is one of three houses he owns. It's not clear if he's in residence. Reedy was let into the house to see the painting, but that was a couple weeks ago. My assistant called the house and got a machine."

"What's your assistant's name?" I asked Diesel.

"I don't know. She's been with me for three weeks, and it's too late to ask. She'd get insulted and quit."

"So how are we going to get in to see the painting?"

"We ring the doorbell. If someone answers, we lie our way in. If no one answers, we break in."

"I don't like either of those ideas."

Diesel parked two houses down. "What's *your* plan?"

"You treat me to dinner at a nice restaurant, we go home, and we pretend we didn't discover the computer printout of the second painting."

"Not gonna happen, but after we break into the house, I'll buy you a pizza and a beer."

"I'm not breaking into the house. Look at these places. They all have alarm systems. The police will come and arrest us."

"No worries. There's not a jail that can hold me."

"But what about me? I can't do the whole Houdini thing you do with locks."

"Yeah, you'd be behind bars for a long time."

"Good grief."

Diesel grinned. "I'm kidding. I'll take care of the alarm."

"You can do that?"

"Usually."

"Only usually?"

"Almost always."

I followed him up the stairs to Belker's house and waited while he rang the bell. No answer. He rang again. Still no answer.

"I have a bad feeling about this," I said. "I don't think we should break in. It's daylight. People will see us."

Diesel put his hand to the door and the lock tumbled. "No one's looking."

He opened the door, we stepped in, and the alarm went off.

"Bummer," he said. "I usually block the electrical signal."

"Shut it off! Shut it off! *Do something*."

"Look around for the painting."

"Are you insane? You set the alarm off. The police are rushing over here."

Diesel was going room by room. "The alarm company will call first."

The phone rang.

"What should I do? Should I answer it?" I asked him.

"No. You don't know the code word. Just look for the painting."

My heart was racing, and I was having a hard time breathing. "I'm gonna go to jail. What'll I tell my mother? Who'll make cupcakes for Mr. Nelson?"

"I found it," Diesel yelled from upstairs, barely audible over the screaming alarm.

"I'm leaving," I yelled back. "You're on your own. I can't eat prison food. It's probably all carbs."

Diesel jogged down the stairs with the painting.

"What are you doing?" I asked him.

"I'm borrowing it."

"Omigod, you're *stealing* it."

"Only for a little while. Help me wrap this bed sheet around it."

"It's huge!"

"Yeah, it didn't look this big in the

book. The gold frame doesn't help, either."

We got the sheet around the painting, and Diesel hustled it out the door and down the street to his car. I had the hood pulled up on my sweatshirt and my face tucked down in case someone was looking and making notes or, God forbid, taking pictures. We slid the painting into the back of the SUV, scrambled into the front seat, and Diesel took off. He turned out of Louisburg Square, onto Pinckney. I looked back and saw the flashing lights of two cop cars as they came in and angle parked in front of Belker's house.

"See," Diesel said. "No problems."

"We missed getting arrested by two minutes. And we've got a hot painting in the back of the car. It's probably worth millions. I mean, this isn't like shoplifting a candy bar. This would be a felony. Remember what they did to Martha Stewart? They put her in jail. I don't even remember why. I think she told a fib."

"Nobody said saving mankind was going to be easy," Diesel said.

"We're *art thieves*."

Diesel looked over at me. "Does that turn you on?"

"No! It scares the bejeezus out of me. Aren't you worried?"

"No, but I'm hungry."

CHAPTER NINE

We retrieved Carl from Diesel's apartment, got take-out pizza in Marblehead, and brought it back to my house. Diesel hung sheets and towels over my kitchen windows so no one could look in, and we propped the painting up against a wall.

"It's nice," Diesel said, working his way through a piece of pepperoni with extra cheese, "but it's just branches and flowers to me. I'm not seeing any clues."

"Reedy thought you had to believe in true love to see the clue."

Diesel took another piece of pizza.

"I've gotta be honest with you. I don't even know what true love means. If it wasn't for John Lovey living in the nineteenth century, I'd think the whole true-love thing was invented by Disney."

I'd been staring at the painting for a half hour and I didn't see any clues, either. I looked at it up close, and I looked at it far away. I looked at it with one eye closed. I examined the back. Nothing. But when I touched it, I felt the energy.

"Do you see a clue?" Diesel asked me.

"No."

"Hunh," Diesel said.

"What's *hunh* supposed to mean?"

"Looks to me like I'm not the only one who's cynical about true love."

I sunk my teeth into a piece of pizza. "I'm starting to think John Lovey was a nut."

Diesel gave a bark of laughter and took a long pull from his bottle of beer.

"Eeh?" Carl asked, pointing to the pizza box.

Diesel gave him a second piece and cut a slice off for Cat.

"Do you want me to help read through

the papers you took off Reedy's desk?" I asked Diesel.

"No, but thanks. I left them in my apartment. I'm going to spend the night here watching the game and guarding your body."

"How much of the night are you talking about?"

"The whole night. All of it. And then some."

This was a real dilemma. I didn't want another Wulf encounter in the middle of the night, but I also didn't want a Diesel episode in the middle of the night.

"The *whole* night might not be a good idea," I said. "It's, you know, awkward."

That got another smile. "Afraid you can't keep your hands off me?"

"It's not *my* hands I'm worried about."

"Better my hands than Wulf's hands," Diesel said.

"That's true, but it wasn't the answer I was hoping to hear."

The game was in overtime when I went to bed. I brushed my teeth and went with the least seductive outfit I could find . . . a lightweight T-shirt and black Pilates pants. I crawled into bed, and Cat took his position at my feet. I shut the light off, and heard Diesel on the stairs.

"Bruins won," he said, coming into the bedroom, carting the Van Gogh with him.

"What's with the picture?"

"I didn't want to leave it downstairs where it could get snatched."

"You could have slept downstairs with it."

"I don't fit on the couch."

"You don't fit here, either."

"True. But I fit *better*."

Carl looked over the edge of the bed. "Eep?"

Cat rotated his head and looked slitty-eyed at Carl. Cat wasn't big on sharing his bed with a monkey. Probably, he wasn't crazy about sharing it with Diesel, either.

Carl inched his way around the bed to the point where he was farthest away from Cat, carefully climbed onto the bed, and sat hunched, trying to make himself small.

"Does Carl sleep with you when you're home?" I asked Diesel.

Diesel stripped his T-shirt over his head and kicked his shoes off. "No. He has his own bedroom. You only have one bedroom, so he doesn't know where to sleep."

"Like you."

"Honey, I know exactly where to sleep."

His jeans hit the floor, and I told myself to look away, but I couldn't force myself to do it. Diesel naked was a masterpiece of male perfection. I was tempted to turn the light back on, but I was afraid that would be too obvious. He dropped his boxers and slipped under the covers next to me.

"This thing that happens when two people with special abilities get together. You want to explain that to me again?" I said to him.

"One of them loses all their special abilities. No way of knowing ahead which one will be the loser."

"And just exactly what is it that triggers this power outage? I mean, does there have to be penetration? Does there have to be an exchange of body fluids?"

"Exchange of body fluids is a given, beyond that it's a gray area."

"How about contraception? A condom would contain body fluids. What then?"

I could feel Diesel smile. "You want me bad."

"I do not! That's ridiculous. I'm just asking."

He slid his arm around me and nuzzled my neck. He was warm, and he smelled great, and I liked the way he felt pressed against me.

"How about we just fool around a little," he said.

"Is that allowed?"

"Probably."

"Is that probably like the *I probably can defuse the alarm system*?"

"Yeah, it might be similar."

I heard rustling in the dark room and realized Carl was creeping across the bed, trying to get closer to Diesel and me, trying to find a place to sleep. At the same time, there was movement at the foot of the bed. Cat was uncurling, slowly stalking Carl.

"Maybe you can find a place for Carl to sleep," I said to Diesel. "I don't think Cat likes having a monkey in his bed."

"They're fine," Diesel said. "They'll figure it out."

"Yes, but . . ."

YEOWL.

EEeeeee!

Cat pounced on Carl, and Carl went postal. There was a lot of screeching and hissing and growling and monkey bitch slapping. I dove under the covers, and I felt Diesel roll over me. I peeked out and saw he had Cat and Carl by the scruffs of their necks, holding them both at arm's length.

I switched the light on, and Diesel marched out of the room, still holding Cat and Carl. Minutes later, Diesel returned to bed and shut the light off.

"Is everything okay?" I asked him.

"I have Carl on the couch in the sleeping bag, and Cat is in his bed in the kitchen."

"Was anybody bleeding?"

"Not that I could see." There was a

beat of silence. "Now that I'm back in bed, would you like me to demonstrate some of the things we shouldn't be doing?"

"No!"

Carl and Cat had saved me from doing something stupid. And it had the added bonus of seeing Diesel with the light on. Sweet dreams tonight.

I was snuggled into Diesel when I woke up. He was still asleep, so I carefully eased away from him and shut the alarm off before it rang. Cat had returned to the foot of the bed. No sign of Carl. I grabbed clothes and tiptoed into the bathroom. I showered and dressed, and Cat and I went downstairs.

Four hours later, I was in the bakery kitchen helping Clara make meat pies and Diesel strolled in, carrying the painting wrapped in the bedsheet.

"I need you to babysit this," Diesel said. "There's a problem I have to solve, and I don't want to leave this unguarded in your house."

"Put it against the far wall and make

sure it's covered. I'm up to my elbows in bread dough and meat filling here."

"I'll be back before you leave today," Diesel said, propping the painting against the wall. "Call me if there's an issue."

He went out the back door, closing and locking it behind him.

"What's under the sheet?" Clara wanted to know.

"A painting. We sort of borrowed a Van Gogh yesterday."

"A real Van Gogh?"

"Yeah."

"Borrowed?"

"Yep."

"Borrowed what?" Glo asked, coming in from the front shop.

"A painting," Clara said. "It's under the sheet."

Glo pulled the sheet away, and we all looked at the painting.

"It looks like wallpaper," Glo said. "My grammy had wallpaper like this in her bedroom, but it wasn't 3D."

"What do you mean 3D?" I asked.

"Well, there's the branches and flowers, and then in front of them, there's writing and some bells with numbers and musical notes, and then a man's name."

"I don't see any of that," Clara said. "You haven't been smoking mushrooms, have you?"

"No," Glo said, "but I had some on pizza a couple days ago."

"What does the writing say?" I asked her.

"'Hope endures in the reader of this message. Love comes to those who still hope,'" Glo said. "I'd like to think that's true, because I haven't had great luck so far in the love department."

"Yes, but you're such an optimist," I told her. "Every time you meet a man, you're sure he's going to be your perfect match."

"What else do you see?" Clara asked. "You said there were bells and a man's name."

"Charles Duane."

"Draw a picture of the bells, so I can see them," I said to Glo.

"Sure, but they're just plain old bells that are numbered one through nine." Glo's eyes went wide. "This is about saving mankind, isn't it? I bet this is some kind of clue to finding the Luxuria Stone. And I'm the only one who can read the clue. This is definitely a sign of wizardry. This is *so awesome*."

"The clue is only good if you can figure out where it takes you," Clara said. "Just reading the clue isn't enough."

"True," Glo said. "But I still feel special. And I'm sure we'll figure it out."

I returned to the meat pies, and Glo sketched the bells on a napkin and went back to tending the shop.

CHAPTER TEN

Diesel called at noon and said he was having problems. "My boss has me looking for a guy named Sandman. He's one of us. His specialty is putting people to sleep and robbing them."

"One of us?"

"That's what I'm told. In the registry, his ability is listed as mid-level metal bender, but clearly he has something new with the sleep thing."

"There's a registry?"

"Yeah. That's how I found you. A lot of people slip through the cracks, but for the most part, it's all documented."

"How?" I asked him.

"Don't know. Don't care. I just do my job, and after twenty years of service I can retire, and I'll have my own island in the South Pacific."

"Where's all this going?"

"I can't find him," Diesel said. "He's not where he's supposed to be. Take the painting with you when you leave work, and I'll hook up with you later."

I cleaned my area, wedged the painting into the backseat of my car, and headed for home. I had my radio tuned to a news station, and they were talking about an art theft. A rare Van Gogh had been boldly stolen in broad daylight from a Boston town house. No one saw the robbery take place. The owner was overseas at the time.

I wondered how such a thing could happen . . . a robbery like that in broad daylight. And then I realized they were talking about the Van Gogh I had in the backseat. Good God, *I* was the one who'd committed the robbery.

I had a moment of dizziness, followed by nausea. Stay calm, I told myself. Don't panic. It's not as bad as it sounds.

The painting wasn't actually stolen. It was *borrowed*. Probably, I wouldn't have to do more than ten years for borrowing. Time off for good behavior might have me out before I turned forty. A sob inadvertently escaped from somewhere deep in my chest, and I changed the radio station to seventies rock.

I parked in front of my house and hustled the painting inside, being careful not to let the bedsheet slip away. I locked the door behind me, carried the painting upstairs, and slid it under my bed. Out of sight, out of mind. Except it wasn't totally out of my mind.

"This is a mess," I said to Cat. "What if I get caught? What will I say? *I'm sorry, your honor, but I was trying to save all of mankind*. And then I'll tell the court I'm special because I can identify bewitched objects. Even *I* don't believe it."

I sat on my couch with my computer and Googled Charles Duane. I assumed he was a composer, since his name seemed to be attached to the musical notes on the painting. I was surprised to see he was the rector of the Old North Church from 1893 to 1911.

"This does me no good at all," I said to Cat.

The doorbell rang and my heart jumped in my chest. I peeked out my front window, fearing a SWAT team, seeing Glo instead.

I opened the door to her. "Why aren't you at work?"

"Clara said I was useless, so she gave me the afternoon off. She said she didn't want to hear any more about saving the world, but golly, it's important. I mean, it's the *world*. And you'll never guess what I found out. Charles Duane was the rector of Old North Church, so let's go."

"To Old North Church?"

"I'm sure we'll find more clues there," Glo said. "My wizardry is finally kicking in. I wouldn't be surprised if we get there and I have a vision. I might be able to point us right to the Luxuria Stone."

I put Cat in charge of guarding the hidden painting, and an hour later, we were at Old North Church in Boston's North End. It's a sturdy, blocky redbrick building with a bell tower that looks like it was built by Practical Pig. The sidewalk and courtyard surrounding the church are redbrick, and all the other buildings on Salem Street are also redbrick. There's parking on one side of the street with enough space left for a single car to navigate the remaining blacktop patched road. Across the street from the church is an Italian café and a shop selling T-shirts to tourists.

I'd walked the Freedom Trail a couple months ago and stopped in to see the church, so I knew something about it. Built in 1723. It's an Episcopal church with services on Sunday. Other days, it's open to the public as a national treasure with tours and a gift shop. The interior is white, with some dark wood trim and elaborate chandeliers hanging over the center aisle. Pews are set into boxes, and there's also a second-floor balcony with a pipe organ.

"I've never been in here," Glo said, looking up at the chandeliers. "This is so historic."

We were the only tourists in the church. Glo was walking around, reading plaques. I sat in one of the pews and listened to the silence, imagining what it must have been like to worship here two hundred years ago. Someone was working on the balcony level. I could hear footsteps and an occasional *clink*.

"The chandeliers and the bells were shipped here from England," Glo said from the back of the church. "How cool is that?"

A guy looked over the balcony railing at Glo. "Are you interested in the bells?"

"Yes," Glo said. "Can they still ring?"

"We usually ring them for Sunday service. And we have weekly practice sessions."

"Wow," Glo said. "I'd love to hear them."

"I'm one of the bellringers," he said. "If you come back on Sunday, maybe we could go out for coffee after."

"Sure," Glo said.

"I have some questions about the bells," I said to him.

"Give me a minute to finish cleaning up, and I'll be right down."

"How do you always manage to get a date?" I asked Glo. "You're like a date magnet."

"I'm cute," Glo said. "And I think it

must be part of my wizard power. I think to myself, *Boy, he's hot. I'd like to go out with him,* and next thing, I've got a date."

I didn't know about the wizard power, but she was right about being cute. I was sort of cute in a girl-next-door kind of way that didn't seem to encourage dates. Glo was cute in a quirky, fun way that was obviously more approachable. Truth is, I wish I was more like Glo, but I'd feel like an idiot if I tried to wear a pink ballet tutu with green-and-black striped tights and motorcycle boots.

I heard a door close upstairs and the bellringer ambled over to us. He was around twenty. Still in his puppy stage, with long, gangly legs and big feet. Sandy blond hair that had probably been cut by a friend.

"Josh Sidwell," he said, extending his hand.

"Lizzy Tucker," I said, shaking his hand.

Glo stuck her hand out and smiled. "Gloria Binkly, and I've never dated any-one named Josh before. I'm, like, a Josh virgin."

"Jeez," Josh said. "I'm honored."

"How do you get to be a bellringer?" I asked him.

"I'm a member of the MIT Guild of Bellringers."

"Wow, a college guy," Glo said. "I'll bet you've never even been arrested."

"I got caught smoking pot once, but I was underage, and I didn't get charged with a felony."

"Even better," Glo said.

"So tell me about the bells," I said to Josh.

"There are eight of them. They were cast in Gloucester, England, in 1744, and they were hung here in Old North in 1745. They were restored in 1894 and again in 1975."

"Is it possible to play a song with them?"

"I suppose it's possible, but they're not designed to play a song. These are tone bells. We have certain sequences that we play," Josh said. "It's a complicated process."

"This is confusing," I said. "I was under the impression there were nine bells."

"Nope," he said. "Right from day one, there were only eight. Maybe you're thinking about the Duane bell. Charles Duane was a church rector. He was the first rector to have the bells refurbished. He also had a small replica bell made as well and asked that it be buried with him. Sometimes it's referred to as the ninth bell."

"Where's he buried?"

"Here," Josh said. "There are thirty-seven tombs and over eleven hundred bodies buried in the basement."

"That's a lot of bodies to bury in your basement," Glo said.

"They give tours," Josh said. "It's awesome. Charles Duane has a plaque and everything. Not everybody has a plaque."

"Is it creepy down there?" Glo asked. "Are there ghosts?"

"The tour I took didn't see any ghosts. At least, I didn't see any. And it wasn't creepy, except it feels a little claustrophobic."

"Thanks," I said to Josh. "You've been very helpful."

"Are you walking the Freedom Trail?"

"No," Glo said. "We're saving mankind."

"Excellent," Josh said. "See you Sunday."

"He was dreamy," Glo said, when we got back to my car. "He could be the one I've been looking for. He spoke English and everything. I have a good feeling about him."

We left the North End and hit 1A at rush hour. Route 1A isn't good at the best of times. Rush hour is excruciating. By the time I rolled into Marblehead, I was starving and my back was in spasm.

"Remind me to never do that again," I said to Glo.

"If I could just get Broom to cooperate, we could fly," Glo said. "Then we wouldn't have to worry about traffic. Harry Potter didn't have to worry about traffic."

"You realize Harry Potter isn't real, right?"

"Of course, but he *could* be. I mean, maybe not *Harry Potter,* but someone like him. Who's to say?"

Glo had parked on the street in front of my house, and I pulled in behind her.

"You got your car fixed," I said.

"My neighbor fixed it for me. I went out with him once, but it didn't work out."

"He was shot with a nail gun?"

"No. He decided he was gay. He said it wasn't my fault, but I'm not so sure."

We went into the house, and I pulled food out of the fridge. All bakery rejects. Ugly meat pies and stale cupcakes. Glo was halfway through a meat pie and a beer when the back door burst open, and Hatchet jumped into the kitchen, brandishing his sword.

"Vile wenches," he said. "Out of my way whilst I search this keep."

"What's a keep?" Glo asked him.

"You've blacked your windows," Hatchet said to me. "You're hiding something, and I want it."

"Dude," Glo said. "You need to chill. Have a meat pie."

"I will not be dissuaded by your meat pie," Hatchet said. "I want the clue."

"Here's the thing," Glo said. "You're kind of cute. Like, you've got this medieval thing going for you, and it's sort of a turn-on. I mean, I met this other guy today, and he might be the one, but then again it might be you, if you could just get over the bossy part of your personality."

Hatchet lowered his sword. "Thou thinkst I'm bossy?"

"Maybe you're just hungry," Glo said. "Does Wulf feed you? Take a meat pie while I get my book. I was thinking about you last night, and I found a spell that might help."

Glo pulled *Ripple's Book of Spells* out of her canvas messenger bag, set it on the counter, and paged through it.

Hatchet looked at the meat pies. "Dost thou have a ham and cheese?"

I gave him a paper towel and a ham meat pie. "You want a beer?"

"Aye. A tankard of ale would be fine."

"How about a bottle?"

"Whatever," Hatchet said.

"Here it is. I found it," Glo said. "It's a mid-level charm that improves self-esteem. You won't feel subservient to Wulf after I put this charm on you."

"But it is my destiny to be subservient," Hatchet said.

"Piggle wiggle little weewee," Glo read.

"I doest not have a little weewee," Hatchet said. "That is an untruth. An affront to my weewee."

Glo followed along with her finger. "Think large when anger calls, when thoughts are small, when doubt assails, let thy body bloat, release all foul within." Glo reached into her messenger bag and took out a little plastic bag that held a small amount of black powder. She sprinkled the powder onto Hatchet and clapped her hands twice. "Powdered frickberry to seal the deal," she said.

Hatchet sneezed and farted. "Sorry," he said. "I got frickberry up my nose." And he farted again.

"Are you sure you read that right?" I asked Glo. "It sounded more like a charm for intestinal problems than for self-esteem problems."

"I even followed with my finger," Glo said.

I looked at the charm she'd just read. "I think you might have inadvertently changed a word. You said *bloat* and you should have said *float*."

"Are you sure?"

"Pretty sure."

Pbblt. Hatchet farted.

"Maybe you should undo the charm," I said to Glo. "Just say it the right way."

"It's not that easy. I'll have to find the bloat charm and then find the antidote. And that was the last of my frickberry powder. The charm won't stick without frickberry."

Hatchet finished his ham meat pie. "I thank thee for the savory pie," he said. *Bbrrrp*.

"Jeez Louise," Glo said. "You're going to have to take it outside. My eyes are burning."

"Yeah, and I haven't got any clues," I told him. "I'm fresh out."

"I think thou doth fib," Hatchet said, "but I will take my leave for now, as this evil wench hath cursed me with foul flatulence."

Hatchet swooshed out the door with sword in hand, I locked the door after him, and Glo lit a match.

"He was cuter before he started farting," she said.

I ate a meat pie and popped a mini

strawberry cupcake into my mouth. "I suppose we need to send Diesel into the crypt to check out the ninth bell."

"Maybe the Luxuria Stone is there, too. That would be so cool, because we wouldn't have to worry about hell anymore. We could have a kegger to celebrate."

I helped myself to a second cupcake, and Carl scampered into the kitchen, followed by Diesel.

"What's up, little dude?" Glo said to Carl.

"Eeh," Carl said, and he gave her the finger.

Diesel went straight to the refrigerator and got a beer. "That sums up my day, too."

I gave Carl a meat pie and pushed the rest of them over to Diesel. "Couldn't find your bad guy?"

"Eighty-six years old, and he's making me look silly. And I don't think he's even trying. He's so old, he's not giving off any markers. I can't track him. And he's not following a pattern. I don't think the guy sleeps. He just wanders around creating havoc." He took a pie. "What have you been up to?"

"We found the clue that leads to the Luxuria Stone," Glo said. "And I met a really cute guy."

Diesel's eyebrows rose ever so slightly, and he looked over at me.

"It turns out Glo was able to see the hidden message in the painting."

"I'm special," Glo said. "I have hope, and I'm going to find true love."

"The message also contained nine numbered bells. And there was a man's name," I told Diesel.

"Charles Duane," Glo said. "We Googled him and found out he was the rector of Old North Church a long time ago. So we went to the church, and I got a date with the bellringer, and we're just inches from saving the world."

Diesel leaned against the counter and ate his pie. "I have a feeling there's some stuff missing from the middle of that."

"There are eight bells in the bell tower of Old North," I said. "The painting showed nine numbered bells, and we learned that Charles Duane asked to be buried with a small replica bell that's sometimes referred to as the ninth bell."

"I bet there's a secret message on the bell, just like on the painting," Glo said. "Or even better, the Luxuria Stone might be stashed away with the bell and Charlie."

Diesel finished his pie and moved on to a chocolate cupcake. "The perfect ending to the perfect day . . . I get to go grave robbing. Could it get any better?"

"The church is going to be locked," I said. "It'll have an alarm system. And last time, you didn't have such great luck with the alarm. It might be better to go in during the day, when there's no alarm. Glo and I can distract people away from the stairs that lead to the crypts."

"How am I going to get a bell out to the car?" Diesel asked.

"Maybe it would fit in a backpack."

I couldn't believe I was now plotting to steal the bell, when less than an hour ago, I'd almost run off the road in a blind panic over stealing the painting.

"I like it," Diesel said. "I'm comfortable with procrastination. And the Bruins are playing again tonight."

Diesel fills up a house. He's surprisingly quiet, but his energy permeates every nook and cranny. The house feels masculine and safe, although truth is, he probably draws more danger than he scares away. I feel compelled to maintain my independence and shoo him back to his own apartment, but the disturbing reality is that I like having him here.

CHAPTER ELEVEN

Thursdays are usually quiet at the bakery. It was one o'clock and the lunch rush was done rushing. I had the dishwasher loaded and baking trays stacked in the sink for scrubbing. Clara had just put the day's last loaves of bread into the oven. Glo was alone in the shop, reading *Ripple's Books of Spells,* trying to find something that would reverse the charm she put on Hatchet.

We had the door to the kitchen open for air. It was sixty degrees out, with a brilliant blue sky and a hint of a breeze. I heard a car pull into the little back lot, two doors opened and closed, and Diesel ushered an old man into the work area.

The man was about 5'10" and bony. He had pure white hair, beady eagle eyes, and huge old man ears.

"I don't know why I'm getting dragged around like this," he said. "You get to be an age where you should do what you want and not have someone telling you to do this and do that and don't do this and don't do that. You're lucky I'm so easygoing, or I'd be complaining to somebody. I've got rights, you know. And I'm no slouch, either. I can do things. Did I ever tell you I could bend a spoon? Alls I have to do is think about it. How many people could do that one, eh? I could bend a fork, too, but a tire iron is a tough one. I gotta have a good night's sleep before I could bend a tire iron."

"This is Mortimer Sandman," Diesel said. "I'm hanging with him until his son comes to pick him up tonight."

"He's babysitting me," Mortimer said. "Won't let me out of his sight. Like I'm decrepit or something. Thought he was going to offer to wipe my behind in the men's room. Feed me my soup so I don't dribble. How about if you chew my sandwich for me?"

"You tried to sneak away on me, twice," Diesel said.

"Yeah, I'm a real threat for a hotshot like you with all your superpowers. Did I ever tell you about the time I bent three spoons at once? It was at a party, and I just concentrated, and all of a sudden all the ladies' spoons up and bent. You could hear them gasp. I didn't say anything, because that's our code. We don't mention nothing about what we do. I was hot that night. I could have bent anything. Boy, those were the days. I could still bend stuff, but I gotta be careful on account of I got high blood pressure. I don't want to bust a blood vessel over some spoon. It was better back in the day when they were real silver. Softer, more bendable, if you know what I mean. Everything's stainless now. I could get a hernia trying to bend some of them stainless pieces."

"What's the deal with him?" Glo asked Diesel.

"He puts people to sleep, and then he steals stuff," Diesel said.

"So they should stay awake and guard their stuff if it's so valuable," Mortimer said. "How am I supposed to know they want it? You can't even have a conversation with people today without them falling asleep. Sometimes they sleep with their eyes open. I don't know why they don't fall over. If it was me, I'd fall over, but I don't have that problem. I stay awake. I pay attention. I've always been able to pay attention. You gotta concentrate to bend a spoon." He looked over at Clara. "What about you? I bet you can't bend a spoon."

Clara didn't say anything. Her eyes were glassy and her mouth was slack.

"Hey, girly," Mortimer said to Clara. "I'm talking to you. Wake up."

Clara made an effort to focus. "Sorry, I think I dozed off there for a minute."

"How does he do it?" I asked Diesel. "Magic?"

"Boredom," Diesel said. "He just keeps talking, and eventually, your mind turns to the consistency of grits. He lives with his son in Newton, but he ran away from home three weeks ago."

"Why don't you talk about me like I'm not even here," Mortimer said. "What, do I look like I'm deaf? Do you know what it's like to live with my son? It's a mortuary. Why don't I just shoot myself, or jump off a bridge, or drink rat poison. He never does anything. He watches television. What kind of life is that? I need action. I need some hot mamas."

"I found you living in the park," Diesel said.

"I like the park. Lots of fresh air. And people come around in a van and hand out baloney sandwiches twice a day. I like baloney sandwiches. When I was a kid, I always ate baloney sandwiches. I'd take one to school with me every day. My son never eats baloney. He says the stuff in baloney will kill you. I say *when*? I've got cataracts, high blood pressure, enlarged prostate, skin cancer, hemorrhoids, an artificial hip, false teeth, and gas. Every day I take eleven different pills and a stool softener. And now I'm supposed to worry about baloney."

"I thought you were going to save mankind this afternoon," I said to Diesel.

"That's still the plan," Diesel said. "We'll have to take Morty with us."

I had a new batch of rejected meat pies in a bag on my workstation. "Have you had lunch? Do you want a pie?" I asked him.

"I'm good," Diesel said. "I had a baloney sandwich in the park."

"I'll be done in a few minutes," I told him.

"What about me?" Glo asked. "You need me, right? You can't save the world without me. Can you wait until three o'clock? That's when I'm done."

"I don't know what we're doing, but I think we should wait for her," Morty said. "She's a cutie. She makes me want to bend a spoon. Did I ever tell you about the time I bent three spoons at once? I was at this dinner party and . . ."

Clara groaned. "Don't wait until three o'clock. Leave now. *All* of you. If he stays here any longer, I'll go into a coma."

An hour later, we were standing in front of Old North Church.

"I'll go in first," Diesel said. "Give me five minutes to look around, and then all three of you can come in. When you see me go downstairs, make sure no one follows me."

"Oh boy," Morty said. "We're pulling off a caper, aren't we? Now, this is more like it. Don't you worry. No one's gonna get past me and go down those stairs. You can count on me."

"Keep your eye on him," Diesel said to me. "He's sneaky."

"You bet I am," Morty said. "I'm a slippery old bugger. You turn your back on me, and—*whoosh*—I'm gone. Unless I'm with two hot chicks, like you girls, then I might hang around. I'm as old as dirt, but I still got it. One day last month, I almost had a boner."

"The golden years," Diesel said. "I'd like to hear more, but I have to rob a grave. Give me a head start and then come in and cover me."

I watched him walk to the church and go through the red door. I timed five minutes and turned to Glo. "Morty and I will stand close to the stairs that lead down to the crypt. You position yourself more toward the middle of the church. If we see someone who looks official, we talk to them, ask questions, so they don't go near the stairs."

"Gotcha," Glo said. "Let's do it."

A family of tourists stood in the center aisle, staring up at the pipe organ in the balcony. Someone who appeared to be a docent was talking to them and gesturing toward the organ. The docent was a pleasant-looking woman in her fifties. She was wearing sensible shoes, a brown skirt, and a tan sweater set. She had a name tag pinned to her cardigan sweater, but I couldn't see it from this distance.

Morty and I moved toward the stairs, so we screened Diesel while he stepped over the rope that prohibited entry. In seconds, Diesel was out of sight and Morty and I were standing guard.

"What's he after down there?" Morty asked. "It's gotta be something real valuable. Like jewels or a bag of money or a treasure map."

"He's looking for a bell."

"Does it have jewels on it?"

"No, but we're hoping it has a secret message."

"I like the sound of that. This is like Indiana Jones, where he goes into a tomb and he's looking for a clue to something. I don't remember all the details, but there's spiders and a big boulder that could have crushed him, but it didn't. It might not have happened in that order, but it was pretty darn exciting. I've seen all the Indiana Jones movies. And I've seen all the James Bond movies, too. That Bond was a cool cucumber. He knew what to do with the ladies."

A man and a woman came into the church and joined the family listening to the docent. Morty and I pretended to be reading a plaque on the wall. Glo was still hanging in the middle. A couple minutes passed, and two women walked in and went to the docent.

Glo meandered over to me and studied the plaque Morty and I had been pretending to read. "We might have a problem," Glo said. "I've been eavesdropping. There's a crypt tour scheduled. They're waiting for one more person to arrive."

I glanced at the entrance to the stairs. No Diesel. Even with Diesel's skills, it probably wasn't easy to get into Charles Duane's hidey-hole. I saw an older man enter the church and my heart skipped a beat. The tour group was complete. The nine people gathered around the guide, she gave a short speech, and she motioned for them to follow her.

Still no Diesel.

Glo shot me a panicked grimace and pantomimed hanging herself.

"They're going to walk in on Diesel," I said to Morty. "We need to do something to distract them."

"What?"

"You need to have a heart attack."

"I had one of them last year, but I had a stent put in, and now I'm good as new."

"Fake it!"

"Arghh," Morty yelled, staggering forward, lunging at the tour group. "Can't breathe. Got pain." He clawed at the air with one hand, and he had the other clamped to his chest. "I'm having a heart attack," he said, eyes rolling in their sockets, tongue hanging out of the side of his mouth. "It's a big one."

Everyone's first reaction was stunned silence, and then it was utter mayhem.

"Call 911!"

"Who knows CPR?"

"Get him an aspirin."

"Do something!"

Morty crashed into a pew and went down to his knees. "Heart attack!" he said, crawling to the middle of the church. "I'm dying. Somebody help me. I see the tunnel with the light at the end."

Everyone, including Glo, was crouched around Morty.

"Loosen his clothes," someone said.

"Let the cutie do it," Morty said.

I was staring, open-mouthed, at the scene in the middle of the church, and Diesel slung an arm around me.

"He isn't really having a heart attack, is he?" Diesel asked.

"No. They were about to take a tour group into the crypt. This was the best we could come up with on short notice."

Diesel had his bulging backpack hung on one shoulder. "I have the bell. You need to rescue Morty before the paramedics show up and take him for a ride."

I inserted myself into the crowd and stared down at Morty. "You look a lot better now," I said to him. "You've got good color back in your face. I think the heart attack must have passed. I've got Dr. Diesel waiting to check you out."

"Dr. Diesel's here?" Morty asked.

"Yep."

Morty got to his feet. "I don't see the tunnel no more. I must be all healed. In fact, now that I'm thinking about it, I might have had gas."

"Appreciate your concern," I said to the tour group, grabbing Morty by the arm. "Thanks so much for your help. I'll take it from here."

"I'll help get him to Dr. Diesel," Glo said, on Morty's other arm. "Thanks a bunch," she called over her shoulder. "Have fun on your tour."

Diesel was already on the sidewalk when we whisked Morty out the door. A Boston Police car turned onto the street, lights flashing, and we put our heads down and marched off in the opposite direction.

"I should get an Academy Award for that," Morty said. "It's a shame we didn't get to record it. I should be on one of them doctor shows where people die every week. I was an accountant for forty-five years. What was I thinking? I should have been a movie star."

We walked down Salem Street, turned onto a side street, and happened upon a small deserted park. We sat on a bench and looked around. No police. No one paying any attention to us.

"What was it like down there?" I asked Diesel.

"Cramped. Nothing fancy. Mostly brick walls with burial chambers sealed behind cement and small metal doors. Cement floor freshly painted. Fortunately, Duane's tomb wasn't completely cemented over, and the bell was right up front behind the door."

"Was there anything written on the bell?"

"I didn't see anything when I grabbed it."

Diesel pulled the bell out of his pack and held it out for us to see.

"Are you sure you want to bring the bell out in the open like this?" I asked him.

"There's no reason why anyone would suspect this bell came from the church. I put the door back in place, and it should be okay unless someone knocks up against it. With the exception of a little dust on the floor, there's no reason to suspect anything weird happened."

We all studied the bell inside and out, but we didn't see any message. Diesel swished the bell back and forth. *Clang, clang, clang*. No message.

"Touch it," Diesel said to me. "See if it's holding energy."

I put my hand to the bell. "It's warm," I said. "And it vibrates under my touch. I can't say if it's imprinted with a message, but I can tell you it has abnormal energy."

"Maybe you have to play all nine of the bells for the message to surface," Glo said.

Glo was totally into this. Morty was along for the ride. And it was hard to tell what Diesel was thinking. On the one hand, I was having a hard time believing that ringing nine bells would produce a magical message. But then on the other hand, it didn't seem so far removed from television, the Internet, and microwave cooking. Technology and magic were closely aligned in my brain.

"Okay," Diesel said. "Let's go back to the church. I'm having a hard time wrapping my head around a message magically appearing on this bell, but I haven't anything better to contribute."

We went back to Salem Street and walked several blocks to the church. I went in first and looked around. The church seemed to be empty. No tour group. No docent. I motioned for everyone else to come in.

"Now what?" I said.

"There's a bell-ringing room," Glo said. "Upstairs somewhere."

"I'm game," Morty said. "Let's ring some bells."

I looked up at the balcony and beyond. "I hate to be the voice of reason, but I'm sure the bell-ringing room is in the bell tower. There's going to be a long staircase up, and once we ring the bells, that staircase will be crawling with people coming to investigate."

"I know you can bend a spoon," Diesel said to Morty. "How are you with heavy metal? Can you get the bells to ring?"

"Not my gig," Morty said. "I'm strictly a bender. You need someone who could throw a Volkswagen."

The sounds of footsteps and conversation drifted out from the side of the church and the tour group emerged. The docent spotted Morty and gave a gasp of surprise. She left the group and walked over to us.

"Is he all right?" she asked.

"He's fine," I said. "He just needed his medication."

"That was a fright," she said. "I'm surprised to see you back here."

"The truth is, we're fascinated by the bells," I said. "We were hoping there was a way we could hear them ring."

"They rang during practice yesterday," she said, "but they won't ring again until Sunday."

"We'll be gone by then," I told her.

"Isn't there some way we could hear them today?"

"You can hear them electronically. We have an interactive display in the gift shop, and you can also hear them online if you go to the bellringers' website."

"Thanks," I said. "We'll try the gift shop."

"So happy to hear you're feeling better," she said to Morty. And she returned to her group.

We left the church and walked next door to the gift shop. The interactive display was next to shelves of miniature bells, books about the bells, and CDs. The display on the touch screen showed eight bells and gave a description of each one. I touched bell number one and it played a bell tone. The tone for number two was slightly different. There were several people browsing in the store. No one looked our way.

Diesel took the bell out of his pack and held it in front of the display. "Play all eight of the bells," he said to me.

I played the bells on the screen, and we watched Duane's bell.

"Anybody see anything?" I asked.

Everyone shook their heads no.

Diesel made the bell *clang*. Still nothing.

I had Glo's drawing with me. I pulled it out of my pocket and looked at it. "The bells aren't numbered consecutively," I said. "The number three bell gets played first."

I played the bells according to the napkin, Diesel *clanged* Duane's bell, and we all held our breath as words appeared on the bell. *The silence often of pure innocence persuades when speaking fails. The history often of Tichy persuades when pure innocence prevails*.

Glo pulled a pen out of her tote bag, copied the message onto the back of a gift shop brochure, and gave it to me.

"That was weird," Morty said.

Not so much, I thought. Weird was my new normal.

CHAPTER TWELVE

We met Morty's son in a South End parking lot and handed Morty over. The son seemed nice enough and genuinely relieved to have his dad back.

"No more stealing," Diesel said to Morty.

"Hah," Morty said. "You should talk about stealing."

An hour later, Diesel dropped Glo and me off at the bakery so we could get our cars. "I have to check on Carl," he said. "I'll meet up with you later."

I waved him off and searched in my bag for my keys. The bakery was closed and there were only two cars in the small lot. Clara was obviously off somewhere, probably having a glass of wine with a friend.

"That was really cool the way the writing appeared on the bell," Glo said, unlocking her car. "But I don't get the clue. *The silence often of pure innocence persuades when speaking fails. The history often of Tichy persuades when pure innocence prevails*. What the heck does that mean?"

"I don't know. I was hoping we'd find the stone today, so I could get back to my nice safe life."

Pbbblt.

"Did you do that?" I asked Glo.

"No."

We stood still and listened.

Pbbblt.

"It smells like ham," Glo said. "It must be Hatchet."

Hatchet moved out from the shadows. "My intent was to capture and torture for information, but you have made my job easy. I now know the clue and can give this information to my master."

"He's not going to believe you," Glo said. "You fart."

Hatchet stood tall with one hand on his sword. "Everyone doth fart."

"Not like you," Glo said. "You're a ham farter."

Hatchet pressed his lips together. " 'Tis a manly fart."

"It would be best if Hatchet didn't get to talk to Wulf," I said to Glo.

Glo nodded. "I was thinking the same thing." And she jumped at Hatchet. "Get him!"

Hatchet turned and ran flat-out down the street in the dark, with Glo and me on his heels.

Pfft, pfft, pfft, pfft.

Glo took a flying leap, tagged Hatchet, and they both went down to the ground.

BAROOOOMPH!

Hatchet was kicking and clawing, Glo was holding tight, there was a flash of light, and Wulf appeared.

"Enough," Wulf said.

Glo and Hatchet went flat on their backs and looked up at Wulf.

"Master," Hatchet said. "I have critical information." He went to all fours in an effort to stand, he farted, and I heard Glo squelch a nervous giggle.

Wulf stood still and silent, his attention turned to me. "Tell my cousin he courts anarchy," Wulf said, his voice soft, as always.

I felt a hot flush creep from deep inside me to the surface of my skin. Adrenaline, I told myself, pushing aside the possibility that it felt a teeny bit sexual.

Wulf and Hatchet slipped into a shadow and disappeared. Moments later, a car engine caught and roared down the street.

"That's a ten on my Creep-O-Meter," Glo said, getting to her feet. "How does he just appear and disappear? And what *is* he?"

"I think he's a human."

We walked back to the bakery, carefully got into our cars, locked the doors, and drove off. I reached my house and was relieved when Diesel drove up behind me two beats later.

"I have bad news and bad news," I said to Diesel when we got inside and flipped the light on. "Which do you want to hear first?"

"Am I going to hate this?" Diesel asked. "Is it necessary to tell me?"

"Hatchet overheard Glo talking about the message on the bell, so we're no longer the only ones with that information. And I ran into Wulf, and he said you were courting anarchy."

"What's that supposed to mean?"

I did a palms-up. "He didn't explain it. He disappeared in a flash of light."

"No smoke?"

"Didn't see any, but it was dark."

Cat 7143 rubbed against my leg. He was hungry. I was hungry, too, and I couldn't stand the thought of another meat pie.

"I'm going to pull something together for dinner," I said to Diesel. "I suppose you should do some research." I handed him the brochure with the two sentences Glo copied off the bell. "You can use my computer."

I started rice cooking, defrosted a chicken breast, chopped it up, and dumped it into my wok. I listened to the chicken sizzle in the hot oil and felt better. It was good to do something where I felt in control and had some level of competency. I tossed in diced vegetables, added chili pepper and soy sauce for kick. I would have liked to add cashews or peanuts, but my cupboard was bare. I needed to shop. I set the table for three, and yelled to Diesel that dinner was ready.

Carl got to the table first. He climbed onto his booster chair and sat with excited expectancy. I tied a napkin around his neck and brought him his dinner in a wide bowl. No fork. No spoon. No knife.

"Finger food," I said to Carl.

"Eeeh?"

I picked a piece of chicken out of his bowl and held it out to him. "Eat it with your fingers."

"That's a disaster waiting to happen," Diesel said, taking his seat.

"What do *you* feed him?"

"Hot dogs, peanut butter sandwiches, Cheerios, and mangoes."

"No wonder he likes to eat here."

"Yeah," Diesel said. "For the same reason I like to eat here."

I brought bowls of stir-fry for Diesel and me, and I sat down.

Carl looked at me and carefully selected a piece of chicken from his bowl. "Eeh?" Carl asked.

"Exactly," I said. "Eat it."

"I'm not cleaning up the mess," Diesel said.

"There's no mess. He's being careful."

"I bet you were a pushover in high school," Diesel said. "A guy could probably tell you anything and you believed it."

"I wasn't a pushover until culinary school. I was a late bloomer."

Carl picked out a peapod and ate it. He ate another chunk of chicken. He ate a single grain of rice. He stared into his bowl. He looked at me. He looked at Diesel. He looked back into his bowl. He swiped up a fistful of food and shoved it into his mouth. A few grains of rice fell out of Carl's mouth onto the table. He fisted more food and lost half of it to the floor. He gave the floor the finger, smushed his face into the bowl, and licked it clean. He looked up at me and smacked his lips. "Cha, cha, cha."

"You have rice stuck in your fur," I said.

Carl gave me the finger, jumped off his booster chair, walked into the living room, and turned the television on.

"Does he know that's rude?" I asked Diesel.

Diesel forked into a piece of chicken. "It's hard to tell what Carl knows."

"Are you making any progress on the latest message?"

"We're back to Shakespeare. *The silence of pure innocence persuades when speaking fails* is a quote from *The Winter's Tale*. Basically, it means sometimes silence speaks louder than words. The second sentence references Tichy."

Diesel got up and returned with a notepad.

"Peder Tichy was a Danish paleontologist, geologist, and engineer," he read. "Born May 11, 1790. Died March 17, 1862. He grew up in Copenhagen and, after emigrating to the United States, became a professor of natural history at Harvard."

"Interesting but not helpful."

"He was a pretty influential guy. There

are a bunch of landmarks around Boston named for him. There's a neighborhood in Cambridge called Tichytown, a town in Northern Algeria named for him, and a dinosaur resembling Stegosaurus named Tichasaurus Armatus."

"If the next clue is in Algeria, you're on your own."

"I thought we'd start with the landmarks. I have four, and they're all in Cambridge."

"Tonight?"

"No. Tomorrow. It'll be easier in daylight. And I have a date tonight."

This produced an instant sick feeling in my stomach. The guy who slept next to me naked last night had a date. And it wasn't with me. Okay, so nothing actually happened between us, and he had every right to see other women, and it wasn't like he was my boyfriend. So why did I feel like someone just stuck a fork in my heart?

He stared down at his empty plate. "Is there dessert?"

"No."

"Jeez," he said. "I was just asking."

"Sorry. I guess that came out snappy. I have ice cream."

"Ice cream would be great."

I had vanilla, chocolate, and coffee ice cream. I knew chocolate was his favorite, so I brought him coffee. I wasn't liking him a whole lot.

He finished his ice cream and checked his watch. "I have to run." He pushed away from the table and kissed me on the top of my head. "I'm leaving Carl here."

And he was gone.

"Scumbag!" I yelled at the closed door.

Carl turned the television up a notch.

"And you better watch your step," I said to Carl, shaking my finger at him. "You're on thin ice."

I collected the dishes and huffed off to the kitchen. I was such a dope. I should never have brought him ice cream. Let him get his own dumb ice cream. And he wasn't sleeping in my bed tonight, either. Let him sleep in *her* bed. Okay, that was unrealistic. I had no way of keeping him out of my bed. He just unlocked the door, dropped his boxers on the floor, and sneaked under the covers. Not to mention, I had no way of knowing if he was seeing other women. It wasn't something we discussed. And it would be logical to assume a guy with that much testosterone would want to deposit it somewhere once in a while.

"Men!" I said, dumping the dishes into the dishwasher.

Cat 7143 was sitting on the counter with his half-tail curled around him.

"My life is confusing," I said to Cat. "I can't get a grip on it. And I'm ridiculously attracted to an idiot."

Cat blinked and I took that as a suggestion to have a glass of wine. I cleaned the kitchen, had a second glass, and trudged upstairs. I shucked my clothes and dressed for bed in sweatpants, sweatshirt, and thick socks. I couldn't keep him out of my bed, but I could insulate myself from him.

I was wide awake and sweating like a pig in my insulation when I heard Diesel come home. It was ten o'clock. Not an especially long date. He came into the dark room, kicked his shoes off, and disappeared into the bathroom. He returned in a couple minutes, and the rest of his clothes hit the floor. He slipped under the covers and went dead still for a couple beats.

"What the heck are you wearing?" he asked.

"Workout clothes. I was cold."

"Well, you're not cold now. You're lying there in a pool of sweat."

"I might be coming down with something."

"Me, too. I'm coming down with a strong desire to relinquish my power and spend the rest of my days in the park, eating baloney sandwiches."

"Did the date not go well?"

He covered his eyes with his hands and groaned. "Hideous. She gave me a migraine."

"Why are you dating someone who gives you a migraine?"

"I'm not *dating* her. She called and wanted to see me."

I was getting a strange feeling about this. "Are we talking about anyone I know?"

"Deirdre Early. I told you I was going into town to see her."

"No you didn't."

"I yelled it to you when I got off the phone with her. You were in the kitchen."

"I didn't hear you."

I wanted to get out of bed, take all my clothes off, and do a happy dance, but I restrained myself.

"What did she want?" I asked Diesel.

"Mostly information. She's definitely after the stone. I don't know if she's always been after it, or if she learned about it from Reedy. She's one of us, but she's not in the registry, and I can't pinpoint her power. She brushed it off when I mentioned it."

"And she gives you a migraine."

"Yeah. I have heightened senses, and that includes a sensitivity to power. She's got a lot of it, and it's all negative." He wrapped an arm around me. "You have a lot of power, too, but it's positive. You feel like sunshine."

"Wow."

He was pressed against me, his lips brushing my ear. "What do I feel like?"

"Um, solid."

"I'm more solid than usual," he said.

"I get turned on by women in workout clothes."

"I could take my clothes off, if that would help,"

"Not a good idea right now," Diesel said.

CHAPTER THIRTEEN

It was ten in the morning, and Glo had *Ripple's* open on the counter. "I think I found a spell that will fix Hatchet. It's a general *undoing* spell. It's like one of those programs you run in your computer to get rid of a virus."

"Are you sure his problem is a spell?" Clara asked. "Have you considered the possibility that he needs to change his diet?"

"I guess that's something to think about," Glo said. "The spell could have been a coincidence. Still, it wouldn't hurt to try my new spell out on him. I know he has some aggression issues, but he's kind of interesting. I've been following his blogs and tweets. He knows a lot about old castles and poison and medieval torture."

"Lovely," Clara said. "What every woman looks for in a man."

"He might be stopping in this morning for me to de-fart him. Just don't let him touch anything edible, and keep him away from sharp objects," Glo said.

A half hour later, Hatchet walked in. He was wearing a black-and-silver tunic, black tights, and beat-up Nike running shoes. He had his sword at his waist, and he looked like he was seven months pregnant.

Mrs. Weintraub was selecting a dozen cupcakes for a birthday party when Hatchet got in line behind her and farted.

"I'll take six chocolate and six strawberry," Mrs. Weintraub said to Glo, pretending not to have noticed Hatchet.

Brrrrrrp.

Mrs. Weintraub sneaked a peek over her shoulder and saw that the noise was coming from a medieval minion. This was unusual, because most of the crackpots in Salem were dressed like witches and werewolves.

"Goodness," Mrs. Weintraub said.

"Pardon my flatulence and bloat, good woman," Hatchet said. "A curse has been set upon me."

Glo handed Mrs. Weintraub her box of cupcakes. "No charge," Glo said. "You should leave before they suck up the farts."

"Farewell," Hatchet said to Mrs. Weintraub.

"You gotta learn to control yourself," Glo said to Hatchet.

"I need not control. I need *relief* from this vile bag of gas and stench."

"I hear you," Glo said. "I think I found something. It's a broad-spectrum antidote to whatever ails you. Stand in front of the counter and do what I tell you."

Hatchet stood at attention.

"Begone, begone all manner of enchanted suggestion," Glo read. "Evil eye and witches brew, charmed touch, tainted blood, foul drugged sleep forever leave this vessel, this Hatchet." She snapped her fingers twice. "Turn around three times and clap your hands once," she said to Hatchet.

Hatchet turned around three times and clapped his hands once. We watched and waited. Two minutes passed. No fart. We all breathed a sigh of relief.

"It worked," Hatchet said.

"I was supposed to seal the deal with powdered frickberry, but it's on back order, so this might not last forever," Glo said to Hatchet. "Just come back if you need a refresher spell."

"Very well, but before I take my leave, I must purchase a red velvet cupcake."

Glo put one in a bakery bag and passed it over to him. "Sorry about tackling you last night, but you shouldn't have been eavesdropping. That's really rude."

"My master is on a holy quest, and I am honor bound to help him in any manner."

"Has he figured out the riddle yet?" I asked.

"None of thou's beeswax," Hatchet said. "But I will say this . . . we will succeed where you will fail. And now I must be off to do my master's bidding."

We watched him swish out the door with his bakery bag, and Clara lit a scented candle and sprayed the shop with air freshener.

"That was impressive," I said to Glo. "The reverse spell worked."

"It would have been even better if I'd had the frickberry. And I was supposed to throw a pinch of ground salamander tail over my shoulder when I read about the tainted blood, but obviously it wasn't important."

"Oh boy," Clara said.

"It wasn't as if he *had* tainted blood," Glo said. "At least, none that I know about."

I returned to the kitchen and finished piping frosting onto my cupcakes. I helped Clara with the bread, and I cleaned my workstation. I looked up and saw that Glo was standing in the doorway. Her eyes were huge and her face was white.

"There's someone here to see you," she said to me. "She said her name was Deirdre Early, and I don't know why, but I feel like I'm having a panic attack. I've never had a panic attack before."

I wiped my hands on a kitchen towel and handed Glo a lemon meringue cupcake. "Take a deep breath and eat a cupcake," I told her. "I'll talk to Deirdre."

The shop was empty except for Early, and I understood Glo's problem when I stood behind the counter. Deirdre Early had a way of sucking the air out of a room, or at least of making a room *feel* airless. Her short black hair was flat and glossy, tucked behind one ear, sweeping across the other half of her face. Her skin was Kabuki white. Her eyes were lined with black kohl. Her lips were fire-engine red. She was dressed in high-heeled boots, skin-tight black leather pants, and a blousy red silk shirt.

"I know who you are," she said to me, her voice soft, barely above a whisper, her eyes fully dilated black. "And I know what you do. And I'm telling you now, if you continue to serve Diesel, I will destroy you. Literally. When I'm done with you, there will only be ashes scattered by the wind."

I went scramble-brain for a beat. I'm not sure what I expected to hear from her, but it wasn't this.

"I can't eliminate *him,*" she said, "but I can eliminate *you*. And he will be worthless without you. So I'm giving you warning. Abandon the search."

And she turned and left the shop.

Glo and Clara were standing in the doorway to the kitchen.

"Whoa," Glo said. "That was harsh."

"Does Diesel know about her?" Clara asked.

I nodded. "Yes. Do you think she would really kill me?"

"She seemed capable," Clara said, "but she chose to warn you."

"I got the same warning from Wulf," I told her.

"They both probably fear retaliation from Diesel," Clara said.

I took my chef jacket off and tossed it into the laundry hamper. "This is crazy. We're all looking for the Luxuria Stone, and at least two people are willing to kill for it. And no one can even be sure it exists or that it holds any power. It's like hunting down the Easter Bunny or the Tooth Fairy."

"What about the hidden messages?"

Glo said. "You have to admit they're magical."

I shrugged into my sweatshirt. "The clues were left by John Lovey and his followers. Probably, one or two had special abilities and managed to program the painting and the bell to respond to a certain energy. I suppose it's a kind of magic, but so are ultrasound and yeast."

"You're so logical," Glo said. "I would be exhausted if I had to think up all these explanations. It's so much easier to believe in magic."

Diesel strolled in from the parking lot. "Magic is convenient."

"You just missed Deirdre," I told him.

"Was she buying cupcakes?"

"No. She came to warn me. She said if I kept helping you, she'd turn me into dust."

"Dust is bad," Diesel said. "It would be hard to put you back together from dust."

"This is serious!" I said.

He hooked an arm around my neck and kissed me just below my ear. "Don't worry. I'm not going to let anyone turn you into dust. And just to make sure you're safe, I'm going to follow you home."

"At the risk of being branded a cynic, I think it's more likely you're following me home because you want me to make lunch."

"Not true, but now that you mention it, lunch would be good."

Diesel ate his sandwich and looked at the map he had spread open on the table. "I've marked off three monuments to Tichy in the Cambridge area. The first is a statue of the guy and it's in a small park. Originally, the park was privately owned by a horticultural group, but three years ago, it was sold and turned into a dog park. The second is Tichy House. He lived there for most of his time in Cambridge, and he died there. It's a sort of museum now. The third is Tichy Street. It's exactly one block long, and it ends with a bronze Tichasaurus Armatus statue, in slightly reduced size, planted on the corner, in front of the building housing the Harvard history department. I thought we'd start with these three places. Just walk around and see if you catch any vibes."

I left Cat 7143 to guard the house. I had the Van Gogh under my bed, and the bell in my clothes dryer. Diesel didn't want to return them until the stone was found. Having stolen priceless artifacts in my house seemed like a ticking time bomb to me, but I saw his point. We didn't want them available to any new treasure hunters.

I was riding shotgun, next to Diesel, and I was enjoying the trip. There was a chill in the air, but the sun was bright, and people were running and biking on the Esplanade path next to the Charles River. We crossed the bridge and cruised up Massachusetts Avenue. Diesel turned a couple blocks before Harvard Yard and followed his GPS through a residential neighborhood. Tichy Dog Park was attached to a larger municipal park with a lighted baseball field. We parked and walked to the statue positioned at the entrance to the fenced-in dog area.

The bronze statue of Peder Tichy represented him as a portly, mostly bald little man with a bulbous nose and double chin. There was a simple plaque at the base of the statue with his name and dates of birth and death. A pack of dogs chased one another in the enclosed space, and dog owners were lined up on a bench, talking, watching the dogs play.

"The history of Tichy persuades when innocence prevails," Diesel said.

"What does that mean? What history is it referring to?"

"Don't know. He had a variety of interests."

I reached out and touched the statue. "I'm not feeling it. No trapped energy."

"Moving on," Diesel said. "The Tichy House is a block from here. We can walk."

Diesel is a big guy with a long stride, and you cover a lot of ground fast when you walk with him. I imagine when he's barefoot on a beach he slows down, but today he wasn't wasting time. We stopped at the front stoop to the house and read the plaque. Again, nothing fancy. *Tichy House. Circa 1850. Open to the public. Donations appreciated.*

The house is on the fringe of Harvard's campus in a neighborhood that I suspect is, to a large extent, faculty housing, just as it was in the 1800s. The homes are modest but sturdy. Not many are as old as Tichy House.

I turned just before going through the house's front door and caught a glimpse of a car as it drove past. It was a beat-up junker, and Hatchet was behind the wheel. He was focused on the road ahead and didn't notice us. Probably running down all the Tichy leads, like we were doing.

The two front rooms of the house held displays of Tichy memorabilia. Framed awards and diplomas, bound professional papers, photographs of Tichy and his family, some personal treasures. Threadbare Oriental rugs covered the wide plank floor. A woman who looked as old as the rugs sat behind a spindle-legged writing desk.

"May I help you?" she asked. "Feel free to look around."

"Is the rest of the house open to the public?" I asked her.

"Yes, but it's not historically interesting. The upstairs rooms are empty. The kitchen and bathroom were renovated in 1957. The last Tichy to live in the house moved out in 1962, and the house was turned over to the Trust."

Diesel and I walked through the house, studied the mementos in the downstairs rooms, left a donation, and returned to our car.

"Next stop is Tichy Street," Diesel said.

"I think that little museum was our best shot at finding a clue, but I touched everything in there, and nothing registered."

Diesel headed back to Massachusetts Avenue. "I saw Hatchet drive down the street just as we were going into the Tichy House. He could have gone through ahead of us and taken something."

"That's a depressing thought."

We traveled the length of Tichy Street and briefly got out and looked at the Tichasaurus Armatus. It was a fun replica, but it wasn't enchanted, and I couldn't find any hidden messages.

"I have one more stop," Diesel said.

"Mount Auburn Cemetery. Tichy's buried there."

"I'm trying to forget I was threatened with death today. Visiting a cemetery isn't going to contribute to my mental health."

"Just think of a cemetery as a history book with grass."

"What about the ghouls and ghosts who live there?"

"No different from anyplace else."

"And your opinion on death?"

"I think it's to be avoided. Beyond that I have no opinion."

"How about life? Do you have an opinion on life? What do you value?"

"Honor, duty, sex, and the NFL. Not necessarily in that order."

"What about love and friendship?"

"Girl stuff."

I rolled my eyes. "Yeesh."

Diesel gave a bark of laughter. "I don't know how you've survived this long, considering how transparent and gullible you are," he said.

I punched him in the arm. "Jerk."

• • •

Diesel followed his GPS southwest, skirting Harvard Square, hooking up with Mount Auburn Street. Mount Auburn Cemetery is for the most part located in Watertown, but its granite Egyptian Revival entrance is in neighboring Cambridge. It's bordered by other cemeteries and by densely populated neighborhoods of the living.

The cemetery was founded in 1831 and was the first garden cemetery in this country. Its 174 acres of rolling hills are heavily forested in parts with native trees and bushes. The graves and monuments are scattered throughout, accessible by a system of roads and meandering footpaths.

Diesel drove into the heart of the cemetery, following instructions from his assistant. He parked on the side of the paved road, and we took a footpath to the Tichy family plot.

Peder Tichy was buried in 1862 on a grassy hillside now shaded by mature oak trees. The granite monuments around Tichy were worn by age and weather, but the inscriptions were still clear, and we went headstone by headstone, reading names, looking for Tichy.

"I found him," Diesel said, squatting in front of a headstone with a cross carved into the top. "Peder Tichy, survived by his wife, Mary, and his children, Catherine and Monroe."

I joined Diesel and looked at the headstone.

"No message," I said.

"None that I can see."

"This is getting old. At the risk of being a whiner, I'd rather be home taking a nap."

A flash of silver caught my eye, and I looked beyond Diesel to a heavily shrubbed area toward the top of the hill.

"I see feet," I said. "In running shoes. They're sticking out of the bushes, and they aren't moving."

Diesel walked up the hill, reached the feet, and stepped into the rhododendron thicket.

"It's Hatchet," he called down to me.

"Is he dead?"

"Unfortunately, no."

I scrambled up to Diesel and watched him pull Hatchet out of the bushes.

"Are you sure you should drag him out by his feet like that?" I asked. "What if he has a broken back or something?"

"His problem, not mine."

I looked down at Hatchet and a wave of nausea rolled through my stomach. Hatchet had a handprint burned into his neck.

"Oh boy," I said. "Why would Wulf do this to his own minion?"

"It wasn't Wulf," Diesel said. "The print is too small."

"I thought Wulf was the only one who could burn people."

"Apparently not."

Diesel prodded Hatchet with his foot. "Hatchet! Wake up."

"Unh," Hatchet said, eyes closed.

Diesel kicked him in the leg.

"Thank you, sire," Hatchet said.

Diesel shook his head. "That's sick."

Hatchet's eyes opened and took a moment to focus. "What?" he said.

Diesel grabbed Hatchet by the front of his tunic and hoisted him to his feet. "That's my question. What happened?"

"I know not. I was investigating the

grave site, and that's all I remember." He touched his neck. "Ow!"

"It's burned," Diesel said. "In the shape of a hand."

Hatchet looked confused. "Why?"

"Did you remove anything from the Tichy House?" I asked him.

"Nay. 'Twas junk and not worth taking."

"That burn's going to blister," I told him. "You need to put some aloe on it." I looked more closely at his face. He had a huge red splotch on his nose and another on his forehead. He scratched the one on his forehead.

"Are you okay?" I asked him.

" 'Tis as if the foul farts have turned to these beastly hives. I rid myself of one plague only to acquire another."

"If you still have them tomorrow, you might want to talk to Glo about it."

Hatchet scratched his leg and his butt. "Might she find some spell to cure this?"

"Maybe," I said. "In the meantime, you could try calamine lotion."

"You have been most kind," Hatchet said, "but I will still smite thee down if I must. I will slice off your ear, run my sword through your liver, boil you in a cauldron of oil if you attempt to slow me on my quest."

"Wonderful," I said. "I'll add that to the list of things I can look forward to."

"I think I doth got carried away with the oil," Hatchet said. "It would be difficult to procure such an amount of oil."

He scratched his crotch and under his arm, and he limped down the hill toward the road.

Diesel and I took one last futile look around, saw nothing that would indicate the presence of a clue, and followed Hatchet.

"I'm pretty sure there weren't any other cars on the road when we parked," I said to Diesel. "How did he get here? And how is he getting home?"

"Methinks we'll find out," Diesel said. "It appears he doth stand by my SUV."

"Where's your car?" I asked Hatchet.

"Stolen," Hatchet said. "This day doth suck."

Diesel took Hatchet's sword so he wouldn't be tempted to run it through my liver, and we loaded him into the back of the SUV.

"Where do you want us to drop you?" Diesel asked.

"Put me in a sack and throw me into the river," Hatchet said.

"Not my thing," Diesel told him. "Pick something else."

"A pharmacy."

Diesel found one on Massachusetts Avenue. He pulled to the curb, gave Hatchet his sword back, and watched him get out of the SUV.

"Do you want me to wait?" Diesel asked.

"Nay. I will find my own way."

Diesel slipped back into traffic, continued down Massachusetts, and called Wulf.

"Yes," Wulf said.

"Hey, cuz, just wanted you to know Hatchet is in the CVS in Cambridge. He's getting ointment for a handprint burn on his neck. And he's without transportation. Someone stole his car."

There was a silent pause and a disconnect.

"Why are you helping Hatchet? Isn't he the enemy?" I asked Diesel.

"Yes, but it annoys Wulf when I'm nice to Hatchet. And I need to protect Hatchet to some degree. Wulf would be more determined to capture you if he didn't have Hatchet."

"We're missing something with Tichy. I don't feel like we're even close."

"The history of Tichy persuades when innocence prevails," Diesel said.

"Maybe we're not innocent enough."

"That's a given for me."

CHAPTER FOURTEEN

Midway through the morning, the bell over the bakery's front door jingled and Hatchet walked in. I was filling one of the large wire breadbaskets in the front of the shop, and Glo was helping a woman select several meat pies. We all gave a start when we saw Hatchet. His face and hands were dabbed with calamine lotion, his scraggly hair was greasy, and he was scratching like a dog with a flea infestation.

"You," he said, pointing to the woman buying meat pies. "Step aside. I need to speak to the witch."

The woman looked at Glo. "Are you a witch?"

"Not exactly," Glo said. "I think I might have some latent wizard abilities, and there's a good possibility my broom is enchanted, but I'm pretty sure I'm not a witch."

Hatchet narrowed his eyes. "What part of *step aside* did thee not hear?" he said to the woman.

"I was here first," the woman said.

Hatchet drew his sword. "Madam, I have hives in dark places, my balls are on fire, and I have little patience. Wouldst you die for your place in line?"

"Hey," Glo said. "You can't talk to our customers like that."

"Do something, witch. Relieve this itch or I will smite thee down. I will cleave thee in two."

The woman turned and ran out of the store.

Clara was in the doorway. "What's going on out here?"

"Hatchet threw a hissy fit and chased Glo's customer away," I said.

Clara squinted at Hatchet. "What's wrong with him?"

"Hives," I said. "The farting stopped, but now he has hives."

"Omigosh," Glo said. "Do you suppose it could be the ground salamander tail?"

"Do you have any with you?" I asked.

"No," Glo said. "I would have to go to the Exotica Shoppe to get some."

Hatchet was clawing at his crotch. "Maybe if I take my clothes off," he said.

"No!" Clara said. "You can't take your clothes off in my bakery. It's not done. There's an ordinance." She turned to Glo. "Get him out of here. Take him to Exotica before he ruins me. Take Lizzy with you."

"I haven't finished my cupcakes," I said to Clara.

"I'll finish the cupcakes. Go with Glo, and make sure he doesn't come back here. Do whatever you have to do." Clara looked me straight in the eye. *"Do anything."*

Glo took Broom and her messenger bag, and we walked Hatchet out of the bakery.

"It's just a couple blocks," Glo said to

Hatchet. "Try to look normal and not scare anyone on the way."

"My cheeks are chafing, and I have hives in my nose, creeping to my brain," Hatchet said.

"Nobody likes a whiner," Glo told him.

"Sorry," Hatchet said. "Wouldst thou like to beat me?"

Glo declined, but I swear I saw Broom twitch toward Hatchet and Glo take a more firm grip.

Nina waved to us from the back of the store when we entered. She was a puff of lavender cotton candy in a gauzy fluffy gown that Cinderella might have worn to a ball, complete with a froth of lavender tulle perched on her head.

"I just got a shipment of Bavarian elf eyelashes," she said. "Very special. Excellent for constipation and removing spells having Irish pixie dust as their main ingredient."

"I'm looking for ground salamander," Glo said. "I did an *undo* spell yesterday, and it *undid* what it was supposed to but it might have produced hives. I thought it could have happened because I didn't use the ground salamander."

Nina shook her finger at Glo. "It's very naughty to cast spells with incomplete ingredients."

Glo pulled *Ripple's* out of her bag. "I thought I'd just do the spell over with the salamander."

"That probably will work, since it was an undo spell," Nina said, turning to a cabinet filled top to bottom with glass jars labeled Dandelion Fluff, Pickled Pigeon Feet, Scented Toadstool, Green M&Ms, Petrified Danish Quail Eggs. "Here it is," Nina said. "Ground salamander. I sell a lot of this. It's useful in so many spells." She measured a small amount out, sealed it in a snack-size plastic bag, and passed it over to Glo.

Glo had *Ripple's* open on the counter. "Here goes," she said.

Hatchet stood in front of her, trying hard not to scratch.

"Begone, begone all manner of enchanted suggestion," Glo read. "Evil eye and witches brew, charmed touch, tainted blood." She took a pinch of salamander out of the bag and threw it at

Hatchet. "Foul drugged sleep forever leave this vessel, this Hatchet." She snapped her fingers twice. "Turn around three times and clap your hands once," she said to Hatchet.

Hatchet turned around and clapped his hands.

"Do you still itch?" Glo asked.

"Yes!" Hatchet said.

"The spell might take a while to kick in," Nina said. She took another jar off the shelf and gave two capsules to Hatchet. "Take this in the meantime."

Hatchet swallowed the capsules. "What manner of magic was this?"

"Benadryl," Nina said.

"Has the frickberry come in yet?" Glo asked.

"Not yet," Nina said. "I'm hoping Monday."

We all walked back to the bakery, and Hatchet stopped at a purple-and-yellow VW Beetle parked at the curb.

"I will take my leave of thee here," he said.

"Omigosh, is this your car?" Glo asked Hatchet. "This is so cool. This looks like a big Easter egg."

Hatchet sighed and slumped a little. "My sword doth barely fit in this vehicle."

"That's because you have such a big manly sword," Glo said.

Hatchet perked up at that. " 'Tis true. My sword is big and manly."

I left on that note, not really wanting to dwell on Hatchet's sword.

Diesel was waiting for me in the bakery. "We need to go back to Cambridge," he said. "I think I know what we were doing wrong."

"I have to work. I have cupcakes to frost."

"Not anymore," Clara said. "He ate them."

"All of them?"

"No. His monkey ate some."

I glanced over at Carl, sitting in the corner with his eyes half closed. "Looks like he overdid it."

"He has no control," Diesel said.

"And you?" I asked him.

"I have control in spades."

"Go," Clara said. "Take the monkey. Save the world."

We all went out to the SUV, buckled

ourselves in, and Diesel headed for the 1A.

"What's the big revelation?" I asked him.

"I think we were investigating the wrong Tichy. I went back to Reedy's papers and found a letter to Lovey from someone named Monroe. Monroe was thanking Lovey for introducing him to his one true love, the woman he was about to marry. And there's a brief mention of Monroe in the Goodfellow diary. Lovey felt that Monroe had a pure and innocent soul. Monroe's last name is never given, but Peder Tichy's headstone said he was survived by his wife, Mary, and his children, Catherine and Monroe."

"Monroe would be more of a contemporary with Lovey. He'd fit the profile better."

"When I started to research Tichy, it was Peder who kept coming up. Not a lot is out there about Monroe, other than his connection to the Boston Society of Natural History. At the time, the Society's museum was located in Back Bay and was known as the New England

Museum of Natural History. In 1951, it moved to its present location on the Charles River and became the Boston Museum of Science."

"The history of Tichy."

"Exactly. When we were at the cemetery, we only looked at Peder Tichy's headstone. I thought it wouldn't hurt to look at Monroe's."

Almost an hour later, we were on Mount Auburn Street and Carl was asleep in the backseat. We entered the cemetery and saw lights flashing on the road ahead near the area where Tichy was buried. We got closer and realized that the road was clogged with police cars, cemetery maintenance vehicles, and satellite news trucks. Diesel pulled onto a cross street and parked, and we went on foot to the grave site.

We moved through the crush of people and stopped a short distance from what used to be Peder Tichy's last resting place. From my vantage point, it looked to me like Tichy was missing. His headstone was tipped over, and there was a big, messy hole in the ground where grass had grown yesterday.

"What's going on?" Diesel asked one of the cops.

"A groundskeeper discovered this when he came to work this morning. Probably some fraternity had a scavenger hunt and it called for a body. You can't imagine the stuff these kids do."

I supposed it was possible, but I was going to look for dirt under Hatchet's fingernails next time I ran into him.

"Look toward the top of the hill," Diesel said.

It was Wulf, standing alone as usual, dressed in black slacks and a black leather jacket. He was unsmiling, watching the scene at the grave site. He didn't look like he'd been digging. He seemed lost in thought, not looking our way, although I was sure he knew we were there.

Diesel leaned close to me. "Monroe's buried one headstone over from Peder. I can read part of the inscription from here. I don't want to tip our hand to Wulf, so casually walk over as if you wanted a closer look at the crime scene, touch the headstone, and see if there's anything unusual about it."

I followed Diesel's instructions and moved closer to the excavation, resting my hand on Monroe's headstone while I stood on tiptoe to better see over the people. I dropped my gaze and studied the stone. It was engraved with his name and the dates of his birth and death. Nothing more. No secret message. No weird vibrations. I returned to Diesel.

"Nothing," I said.

We walked back to the car and left the cemetery.

"Sometimes I get the feeling Wulf is more of an observer than a participant in this search," I said to Diesel.

"Wulf is like a cat, stalking his prey. He watches, he creeps closer, and he pounces."

"I bet he was a sneaky little kid."

"He was strange. Quiet. Competitive. Brilliant."

"How about you? What were you like as a kid?"

"I was a total screwup."

"But you're not a screwup now."

"Honey, I'm one step away from a bounty hunter. I believe in the value of my job, but not everyone is impressed.

I'm sure my parents wish I was in banking like the rest of my relatives."

"Are your parents *special*?"

"My mother is normal. My dad has unique abilities."

"And Wulf?"

"His mother is my father's sister, and she's the high priestess of the family. Very powerful. Not all her abilities have been recorded. I suspect some of them are dark."

"Does she give you a migraine?"

"No, but she makes me uncomfortable."

I checked Carl, still sleeping in the backseat. "I hope he's not dead."

Diesel looked at him in the rearview mirror. "Too many cupcakes."

"Do you think Wulf is the one who dug up Tichy?"

"No. I think someone followed Hatchet, pried information out of him, and then came back at night and went after Tichy."

"Going on the assumption that something was buried with him. Like the bell with Duane."

"Yes, but the more I think about it, the more I'm convinced the clue was referring to Monroe and his association with what is now the Science Museum."

"Maybe we should visit the original museum."

"I checked on it. The building was on the corner of Berkeley and Boylston. It's been sold and renovated, and everything's been moved to the new location."

"The Science Museum! Are we going to the Science Museum? I've never been there. It's got an IMAX, and a planetarium, and a machine that makes your hair stand on end. Glo was there last month on a date. She said it was awesome."

"You get turned on by science?"

"I got second prize in the science fair when I was in third grade. I made a volcano."

A half hour later, Diesel pulled in to the museum parking garage. He found a space next to the elevator, and Carl sat up.

"Eeep?"

"We're at the Science Museum," Diesel said to Carl. "You can't go in. They don't allow monkeys. You have to wait here."

Carl gave him the finger.

Diesel and I got out, Diesel locked the SUV, and we crossed the short distance to the elevator. We got into the elevator and Carl scampered in after us.

"I thought you locked the car," I said to Diesel.

"I did. He knows how to open the door."

"Okay, how about if you put him in your backpack."

Diesel jogged back to the SUV, got his backpack, and stuffed Carl in.

"You have to be quiet until we get into the museum," I told Carl.

Carl nodded his head and made the sign of a zipper across his mouth.

"Are we sure he's a monkey?" I asked Diesel.

"What else would he be?"

"I don't know, but he's not normal."

CHAPTER FIFTEEN

The Boston Museum of Science isn't huge in comparison to the Louvre, for example. It doesn't take all day to see it. We covered the first floor and didn't find anything with clue potential. We were about to go downstairs, and Carl started squirming in the backpack.

"He's probably hot in there," I said to Diesel. "Maybe we could take him out and disguise him as a kid. We're next to the gift shop. I could buy him a shirt."

"It's going to take a lot more than a shirt," Diesel said. "He's hairy and bow-legged, and he has a tail."

"Work with me," I said. "Think positive. Not every kid is Opie Taylor."

I slipped into the gift shop and found a toddler-size shirt with a dinosaur on it, overalls to match, and baby Uggs. I took Carl into the baby-changing room, got him dressed, and held him up to the mirror so he could see himself.

"Eep," Carl said, pointing to the green dinosaur on his chest.

"Dinosaur," I told him.

He looked at his feet in the Uggs.

"Shoes," I said. "You have to wear shoes in the museum."

I set him down. "You can walk, but you have to hold my hand."

"Eep."

I took him out and showed him to Diesel. "What do you think?"

"I need a drink."

"I think he's cute."

"I bet you dressed your cat when you were little."

"Everyone dresses their cat."

We went to the lower level and looked at the dinosaur exhibit. There were several people milling around. One of them was Hatchet, in full Renaissance regalia. He was slowly moving through the room, touching everything, searching for hidden energy.

"Find anything?" I asked him.

He gave a gasp of surprise at seeing Diesel and me, and he looked down at Carl. "What brings thee to this place with your . . ."

"Monkey," Diesel said, filling in the blank. "And he's not from my side of the family."

Hatchet was wearing a large Band-Aid on his neck, a green tunic, brown tights, his hives were gone, and his scabbard was empty.

"Where's your sword?" I asked him.

"I was requested to check it upon entry. I fear my life as a minion in this century is complicated."

Carl tugged at my hand. He wanted to keep moving. He had his eye on Triceratops.

"Did you dig up Peder Tichy?" I asked Hatchet.

"I did not. There was no need."

"*Someone* thought there was a need."

"A beast without our unique talent."

"Beast is a strong word," I said.

"'Tis a beast. I know this as a certainty. And this beast doth destroy with pleasure."

"Eeeeep," Carl said, stomping his feet in his Uggs, pointing to the dinosaur.

"Hey!" I said to Carl. "Chill. I'm having a conversation."

"Does the beast have a name?" I asked Hatchet.

"It does. My master has warned thee."

"Anarchy," Diesel guessed.

"I know nothing more than that," Hatchet said. "Only that it is fearful."

Hatchet moved on, continuing to leave his fingerprints on every surface.

"Do you think there really is a beast named Anarchy?" I asked Diesel.

"Do I think there's a fire-breathing dragon named Anarchy? No. Do I think there's a dangerous lunatic out there calling himself Anarchy? Good possibility." Diesel took Carl over to Triceratops. "Personally, I think calling yourself Anarchy is overly dramatic."

"This from a guy named Diesel."

"I didn't choose the name."

"What name would you choose?"

"Gus."

"Because it's short?"

"Because it's normal, and expectations would be normal. And that would give me an advantage," Diesel said. "Since I'm not entirely normal."

"Do you think Hatchet got the burn on his neck from Anarchy?"

"It's possible. He got it from someone, and it wasn't Wulf."

"Here's a thought. The handprint on Hatchet's neck was small. So maybe it was a woman's hand. Anarchy could be a woman. And if I wanted to stretch it farther, I might wonder if Reedy's mystery date, Ann, is Anarchy."

"I had the same thought," Diesel said. "And she could have killed Reedy. I never got a good look at the handprint."

"Most women aren't that vicious or that strong," I said.

"This wouldn't be an ordinary woman."

"It could be your aunt!"

"Wulf's mother?" Diesel gave a bark of laughter. "I can't see her worshipping anarchy. She's like Wulf. She likes to keep things tidy and under her control."

A docent was standing by a colorful, huge, two-story contraption that had balls rolling along tracks, banging into bells, dropping into whirligigs, being carried up on tiny escalators, and released for a clattering, dinging, bonging journey down. It was all held in place by a sturdy metal frame, and it was electrically powered. The sign said it was an Audiokinetic Sculpture.

The docent was back on his heels, looking bored. People were watching the sculpture, but no one was talking to him. I left Carl with Diesel and crossed the room.

"I love this machine with the balls and the bells," I said to the docent. "Is it new? This is my first time to the museum."

"Its official name is Archimedean Excogitation," he said. "It was designed and constructed by George Rhoads and placed here in 1987."

"I was hoping there might be something here from the original museum on Berkeley and Boylston."

"There's a small kinetic sculpture on a pedestal to the back of this room. It's one of the few remaining exhibits from the old building."

I turned to look at it and saw that Hatchet had made his way around the room to the sculpture and was standing with his nose pressed to the glass, clearly trying to find a way to get into the display case.

"Oh, for Pete's sake," the docent said. "Sir!" he called out to Hatchet. "Stand back from the display, please."

Hatchet took a step back and skulked off to another exhibit.

"We get some real weirdos here," the docent said. "What do you think he's supposed to be in that costume?"

"A medieval minion," I said.

"That's a first for me. I guess it takes all kinds."

"He seemed really interested in the little sculpture."

"That's why they had to put that exhibit behind glass. You have to set it in motion by hand, and people kept wanting to make it work."

"Have you ever seen it work?"

"Yes. It's not that interesting. The ball swings and hits different bells as it loses momentum. That's the whole deal. And one of the bells is broken. It doesn't make any noise. Just sort of a *clunk*."

"Still, it's interesting because it was part of the original museum."

"That's very true. There's a little plaque on it. Most people don't even see it because it's inside the case."

I went to the display and looked inside at the plaque. *Motion Machine by Monroe Tichy, 1890*. I touched the case with my fingertip and felt a small vibration and some heat. I was sure Hatchet had felt it as well.

Diesel and Carl joined me and looked at Monroe's machine.

"I can feel a vibration," I said to Diesel, "and the docent said there's a bell that doesn't ring. That could relate to the first part of the riddle that says silence speaks louder than words."

"And it's sealed up in a glass case, in a museum," Diesel said. "Why isn't anything ever easy?"

"Maybe the message will be revealed to us if we set the ball in motion," I said to Diesel. "Can you get it to move? You know, *think* it to move or something?"

"That's not in my skill set. I can't make a cow fly, either."

We stared at the display some more. The Motion Machine looked like something you might find in Sharper Image. One of those desktop gizmo presents for people who have everything.

"Unlocking things is in your skill set," I said. "Can you open the case?"

"Yep. It has a little lock on the bottom where it's attached to the pedestal. It's similar to the kind of lock you find on jewelry cases in department stores. Problem is, what happens when I get it unlocked?"

"I guess you steal it."

"Do you have a plan for that, too?"

"Carl and I will create a diversion, you put the Motion Machine in your backpack and walk out with it."

"And what happens if I get caught?"

"I'll swear I never saw you before in my life."

"I guess it could work," Diesel said.

"And if not, you can let yourself out of prison."

"That's cold," Diesel said.

I smiled at him. "If you don't get caught, I'll be nice to you tonight."

His eyebrows rose ever so slightly. "How nice?" he asked.

"*Very* nice."

"Will you come to bed naked?"

"No, but I'll make you cookies."

He grinned back at me. "No deal. If I pull this off, you have to come to bed naked."

"That might encourage me to make sure you get caught."

He shook his head. "You can't do that. We have responsibilities."

"Wouldn't it be frustrating for me to come to bed naked?"

"I can deal."

Yeah, I thought, but what about me? I could barely deal with all my clothes on.

"We'll see," I told him. "Try not to get caught."

Diesel put his hand to the bottom of the case and moved his fingers across the little silver lock. "Done. Your turn."

I looked down at Carl. "You need to create havoc in here," I said. "We don't want anyone looking at Diesel. And when I whistle, I want you to get out of the building and go to the car in the parking lot."

"Chee," Carl said. And he gave me a thumbs-up.

There were about twenty people in the area, plus the docent. Carl scampered across the room, snatched a woman's purse, and ran off with it.

"My purse!" the woman shrieked. "The hairy kid took my purse."

Everyone turned to the woman and then to Carl. Carl held the purse over his head and chattered. "Chee, chee, chee!"

"That's not a kid. It's a monkey!" someone said. "Grab him."

The docent was on his phone, asking for security, and everyone in the room ran after Carl. Mothers, fathers, kids, and an old lady in a motorized scooter chased Carl.

Carl climbed Excogitation, got to the top, and dumped the contents of the purse. Metal balls were running on their tracks, ringing bells, swirling in baskets . . . and tissues, lipsticks, spare change, and assorted female junk rained down.

I'd been the one to set Carl loose, but I was as transfixed as everyone else, watching him swing from the thirty-foot sculpture like a monkey in the wild.

I looked over at Monroe's Motion Machine and saw that it was gone, along with Diesel. The glass display case appeared perfectly intact but empty, and I thought it might take a while for anyone to notice the sculpture was missing. I speed-walked to the elevator and whistled for Carl. He leaped from Excogitation to the spiral staircase, scurried around two guards, dodged Hatchet, and catapulted himself into the elevator just as the doors began closing. Hatchet was close behind him, face red and snarly.

"It's gone," Hatchet said. "The case is empty. I discovered it first, and you stole it, and I *want* it."

He reached out to grab me, instinct took over, and I kicked him in his medieval nuts, knocking him back a couple feet. He let out a *woof* of air, doubled over, and the elevator doors closed shut.

"Eek," Carl said.

"He's a bad man," I explained to Carl.

We departed the elevator at garage level and hustled to the SUV. Diesel was waiting with the motor running. We got in, and Diesel drove out of the garage.

"That was easy," Diesel said.

Easy for him, maybe. Not so easy for me. My heart rate was still at stroke level, and I had so much adrenaline in my system I was vibrating.

"Did you see Carl?" I said. "He was amazing. It was like Cirque de Soleil at the Science Museum. We could get him a job as a Romanian acrobat."

Carl found a cupcake crumb in his chest fur, picked it out, and ate it.

CHAPTER SIXTEEN

Diesel parked and we all trooped into my house and went to the kitchen. Cat 7143 and Carl sat back on their haunches on the kitchen counter, and I stood near while Diesel took the Motion Machine out of his backpack and set it on my work island.

"I had to partially disassemble it to get it into my backpack," Diesel said, "but it was simple. Monroe designed this to be taken apart and put back together."

It was a simple contraption composed of four wooden dowels stuck into a rectangular mahogany base. There was a crosspiece between two dowels at one end, and another crosspiece between the two dowels at the other end. A dowel ran lengthwise between the two cross dowels, and a silver ball and four silver bells hung from piano wire attached to the long dowel. The idea was to set the ball in motion so that it rang the first bell, the first bell rang the second bell, the second bell rang the third bell, and the third bell rang the last bell.

We examined every piece of the machine while Diesel reassembled it, but we couldn't find a message.

"It's all together," Diesel said, securing the last dowel. "Let's see how it works."

He set the silver ball in motion, it hit the first bell with a pretty *ding,* the first bell hit the second bell with a lower-register *dong,* the second bell hit the third bell with a muffled *kunk,* and the third bell hit the fourth bell, producing another pretty chime.

"The third bell doesn't ring," I said.

Diesel got a soda from the refrigerator. "You try it."

I set the ball in motion and got the same result. The third bell didn't ring, and no magic message appeared. I touched each of the bells and got heat and vibration from only the third bell.

"The third bell is definitely charged with a different energy," I said. "We just have to figure out how to set it free."

"Maybe we need Glo," Diesel said.

I called Glo, asked her to come over, and I made grilled cheese sandwiches while we waited. We stood in the kitchen eating our sandwiches, taking turns with Monroe's Motion Machine.

"It's clever," I said.

"It would be even more clever if it gave us the next clue."

"Someone, probably Lovey, had a very unique talent."

Diesel finished his sandwich and put his plate into the dishwasher. "I don't know of anyone today who can duplicate this. These objects were programmed to respond to a basic personality characteristic, like believing in true love. Or in the case of the church bells, to respond to a specific tone played in a prescribed order. That's very different from spewing out enough energy to bend a spoon or open a lock."

"It's magic."

"Magic is something you don't understand and can't explain. But yeah, it's magic," Diesel said.

Cat ate half a grilled cheese sandwich, got bored with the machine, and padded off to look for a spot to nap. Carl stayed fascinated. He was still intently watching the machine when Glo came into the kitchen.

"I know this machine," she said. "They have one exactly like it in a glass case in the Science Museum." Her eyes got wide. "Omigosh, this is it, isn't it? You snitched this from the museum."

"It accidentally got into Diesel's backpack," I told her. "I think there's a clue attached to the third bell, but we can't get it to appear. We thought it might work for you."

Glo set the silver ball in motion and three of the bells sang out, but the third bell only made the soft *kunk* sound. We closely watched the bells for a sign, but nothing happened.

"The history of Tichy persuades when innocence prevails," Diesel said.

Glo giggled. "Guess I flunked that test. It's hard to stay innocent when you're on the hunt for true love."

"In this case, I don't think he was equating innocence with abstinence," Diesel said.

I made Glo a grilled cheese, and she tried Monroe's machine a couple more times, but it was always the same.

"I have to go," Glo said. "I'm meeting the bellringer for coffee tonight instead of tomorrow."

"Thanks for coming over. Sorry to make you go out of your way for nothing."

"No problemo," Glo said. "I was going into Boston anyway, and I got a grilled cheese out of it."

I walked her to the door, waved her off, and went into the living room to watch television with Diesel. I settled next to him on the couch, and I heard the bells chime in the kitchen.

"Carl!" Diesel yelled. "Knock it off with the bell machine. That's museum property."

"I heard four different bells," I said to Diesel.

He hit the mute button on the television.

Ding, dong, dong, ding.

"He never listens to me," Diesel said. "It's like pissing into the wind."

I was on my feet. "Four bells."

We went into the kitchen and watched Carl. He was enthralled with the game, swinging the silver ball, fascinated that it would make the bells chime.

"This is the innocent?" Diesel asked. "A monkey? Are you kidding me? And it's not just *any* monkey. It's my *evil* monkey."

Carl kept his attention on the Motion Machine, but he gave Diesel the finger.

"He isn't exactly *evil,*" I said.

Diesel looked over at him. "He's in the ballpark."

Ding, dong, dong, ding.

"There's writing on the third bell," I said to Diesel. "You have to look closely. It's swirling around it."

Diesel put his hands flat to the counter and studied the third bell. "Those whose minds are shaped by selfless thoughts give Joy when they speak or act. Joy follows them like a shadow."

The writing disappeared, Carl swung the silver ball against the first bell, the bells chimed, and the writing swirled around the bell again. Diesel read it aloud a second time, and I copied it down.

"The *J* in Joy was capitalized," Diesel said. "I imagine that's significant."

"So Joy might be a place."

"Yeah, and I assume it's in the Boston area. All the clues have led us to more Boston- or Cambridge-based clues."

He went to my computer and typed in *Joy Boston*.

"I'm getting a law firm, a camp program, handbags, and a house for sale on Joy Street," Diesel said.

I thought Joy Street sounded promising. It ran perpendicular from Beacon Street up to the top of the hill at Mount Vernon. The Massachusetts State House was on the right-hand side of the street. And Joy was relatively close to Louisburg Square, where we found the first clue.

"I like Joy Street," I said. "I think we should go take a look at it."

"Now?"

"Yeah."

"In the dark of night?"

"Yeah."

Diesel grinned. "You want to do something that will delay going to bed. You're afraid to go to bed because you have to get naked."

"I am not. That's ridiculous."

"If you want to get it over with early, we could get naked now," Diesel said. "Get all that awkward undressing stuff out of the way."

"And then what would we do?"

"Watch television."

"Naked?"

"Yeah. It could be fun."

"No one is sitting on my couch naked."

"Carl does," Diesel said.

That was a disturbing thought.

"I'm going to make cookies," I said. "There's no naked. There's only cookies. Take it or leave it."

"Cookies are good. And I'll eventually get you naked."

"That is *so* arrogant," I said. And so true, I thought.

The bakery is open for a half day on Sunday. People stop in on their way home from church, on their way home from the dog park, on their way home from a morning run, bike ride, power walk. By one o'clock, everyone has gotten their sugar and gluten fix, and the bakery closes.

I slipped out of bed at 4:15 A.M. and tiptoed in the dark to the bathroom. Cat watched me from the foot of the bed. Diesel was still asleep. I took a fast shower, blasted my hair with the hair dryer, and got dressed in my usual outfit of jeans, T-shirt, and sneakers. All was quiet downstairs. Carl was sleeping on the couch. I flipped the light on in the kitchen and got coffee brewing. Cat brushed against my leg, and I bent to pet him. I gave him fresh water and some crunchy cat food.

Monroe's Motion Machine was still sitting on my kitchen counter. It should get hidden away, I thought. Not only was it stolen, but there were other people who would love to get their hands on it. I carted it into my small laundry area, put it in my laundry basket, and covered it with dirty laundry.

I now had a stolen painting under my bed, a stolen bell in my clothes dryer, and a stolen motion machine in my laundry basket. Not a comfortable situation.

I returned to the kitchen, ate a strawberry yogurt, and chugged down a cup of coffee. I zipped myself into a hooded sweatshirt, grabbed my bag, and quietly let myself out. The rest of the houses on my street were dark. It was too early for even the early risers. The air felt frosty, and there was a sliver of moon in the black sky.

I walked the short distance to my car, was about to unlock it, and realized that Wulf was standing very close to me, partially hidden by shadow. My heart stuttered in my chest, and it took a moment for me to regain control.

"I thought you weren't a morning person," I said to him.

"My morning begins at sunrise."

"You aren't a vampire, are you?"

"No," Wulf said, "but I have some similar tastes."

I thought about Diesel, still asleep in my bed, and my line of vision moved from Wulf to my second-story bedroom window.

"If my intent was to take you, we'd be gone by now," Wulf said.

"He'd track you down."

"No doubt."

"So you're here why?" I asked him.

"I was following Anarchy. She tried to recruit Hatchet and failed. He's a fool, but he's loyal. She'll attack you next, and you'll be more vulnerable than Hatchet. I doubt your pain threshold is as high as his."

"Where is she now?"

Wulf went still for a beat, as if he was testing the air. "I've lost her, but I suspect she's not far away. She'll stick close to you, waiting for her moment."

"Why were you following her?"

"She needs to be stopped. My semi-law-abiding cousin isn't sanctioned to destroy her, but I answer to no one."

A light blinked on in an upstairs room across the street. Wulf stepped back into the shadows and silently disappeared.

I thought about going into the house and waking Diesel, but I was running late, and what was the point. I didn't want Diesel attached to me 24/7. And I didn't know what to think about Wulf and Anarchy duking it out.

I got into my car, locked the doors, and drove off, trying to push thoughts of Anarchy out of my head. Much better to think about cupcakes. Plus, it was Sunday, so we would be making apple-cinnamon doughnuts. Okay, so afterward I'd have to clean out the fryer, but it was worth it, because we produced happiness at the bakery. And that was a lot better than *destroying* people. What the heck did that even mean? Was that like a step beyond killing, where you killed someone and then ran over that person with a steamroller or forced them into a paper shredder?

I crossed the bridge into Salem, making the trip in record time. No traffic at this hour on a Sunday. I parked in the lot and hurried into the bakery.

"Sorry I'm late," I said to Clara. "It was one of those mornings."

"No problem," Clara said, adjusting the dough hook on the big mixer. "Everything's on schedule here. I just turned the fryer on, and the dough's rising nicely."

"Does Anarchy mean anything to you?" I asked her.

"Political disorder?"

"This Anarchy is a person. I ran into Wulf when I was leaving the house. He's after a woman named Anarchy."

"I didn't know you and Wulf were so chummy. Isn't Diesel living with you?"

"He isn't living *with* me. He's temporarily camped out in my house. Anyway, he was upstairs asleep, and Wulf was outside by my car."

"Holy cow."

I buttoned myself into my chef coat. "There's something about Wulf that takes my breath away. He's never done anything to actually hurt me, but he still scares the heck out of me."

"He burned you! You have a scar on your hand."

"Aside from that."

Glo walked in, set Broom in the corner, and hung her tote bag on a hook by the door. "I came in early for doughnuts. Who are we talking about?"

"Wulf," I told her.

"He's very hot," Glo said. "He's like a vampire. Dominant and sensual and scary. It's like, have you ever been on the Hulk roller coaster at Universal? It's terrifying and a total rush, and when you get off, your pants are wet and you can't figure out if it's because of this or that."

"Happens to me on the 1A when I have to go around those rotaries during rush hour," Clara said.

I didn't have any comparable experiences to share, so I hauled out a bag of flour and set it on my workstation.

"How was your date with the bellringer?" I asked Glo.

"It was wonderful," she said. "He's so cute. And he's smart. And he knows everything there is to know about bells. I think Broom liked him, too. Broom didn't whack him or anything. I honestly think he might be the one."

CHAPTER SEVENTEEN

It was eleven-thirty, and there were no customers in the shop. Clara and I were done baking and starting final cleanup, and Glo poked her head through the doorway.

"That scary woman is back," Glo said. "The one who feels like Darth Vader. She wants to talk to Lizzy."

"Deirdre Early?" I asked.

"Yes!"

Early's glossy black hair was perfect, swept back behind one ear. Her makeup was dramatic and flawless. Her red knit suit was probably designer, but I didn't know which one. Her demeanor was ice queen.

"We have a problem," she said to me. "I'd like to speak to you in private."

"I'll help Clara," Glo said, escaping into the kitchen.

I kept the counter between us. "What did you want to talk about?"

"You're still assisting Diesel, even after I warned you."

"I'm not assisting him," I said. "We're partners."

"Oh please, look at you. You bake cupcakes. You're nothing more than a minion, like that idiot Hatchet."

"Is there a point to this?"

Her eyes dilated black. "The point is that you have a choice to make. You can be *my* minion or you can die."

"Diesel wouldn't be happy about either of those choices."

"When I get the stone, Diesel will be enslaved to me."

"And Wulf?"

"Wulf as well. Every man and woman on this planet will desire me to the point of insanity."

Oh boy, I thought, she was nutty as a

fruitcake and probably a homicidal maniac.

"You seem like a reasonable person," I said to her. "Why don't you let me give you a box of cupcakes, on the house, and you can go home and think about all this. I mean, you might not want me as a minion. I'm not that good at subservience."

She put her hands palms down on the glass display case and leaned forward, eyes narrowed, face totally drained of color. "Make your choice. My minion or death."

There were assorted bagels on a tray on the top shelf of the case and the bagels under her hands were vibrating.

"Well?" she said.

The bagels were dancing, rattling against the tray.

"Would you mind stepping back?" I said. "You're disturbing the bagels."

The bagels weren't the only things getting disturbed. I was completely freaked. Early was emitting so much energy I was sure my hair was standing on end.

"I demand an answer," she said, raising her voice, her teeth clenched. "I command you to give me an answer *now.*"

She pounded the countertop when she said *now,* and *Zzing . . .* a bagel jumped off the tray and flew the length of the display case.

"Jeez Louise," I said to her. "You need to relax. You're leaking energy. You're going to self-combust if you keep going like this."

Clara came into the shop. "Is everything okay out here?"

"Leave this room," Early said. "This is a private conversation."

"Excuse me? I *own* this room," Clara said.

"I will not tolerate insolence," Early said, her voice a notch below a shriek. She grabbed a heavy glass jar off the counter, threw it at Clara, and hit her square in the forehead. Clara crumpled to the ground, and I went after Early, smacking her on the side of the head with a baguette. She growled and reached for me, and I threw a cherry cheese Danish at her. The cheese Danish caught her mid-chest, leaving a gooey splotch on her suit jacket.

"This is a St. John," Early said, wild-eyed. "You do not do this to a St. John Knit!"

Glo ran out of the kitchen with a ten-pound sack of flour. "I'm pretty sure I've enchanted this," she said, shoving the flour at me. "Hit her with this, and she'll turn into a rock. And then we can bury her, or throw her in the ocean, or something."

I pitched the sack of flour at Early, it hit her in the head, broke apart, and flour spewed everywhere.

"Stand back," Glo yelled to me. "Don't get any of the flour on you, or you might turn into a rock, too."

I jumped away from Early, and Glo and I hid behind the counter, peeking over the top to watch the transformation.

Clara was next to us, kneeling behind the display case, looking ashen with a gash in her head that was dripping blood.

"What the . . ." Early said, taking stock of her St. John Knit suit.

She was covered head to toe with flour, but she wasn't a rock.

"I was in a hurry," Glo said. "I might not have done it exactly right."

Early wasn't moving. She just kept staring down at her suit. I looked at her more closely and realized her eyes were darting around.

"I don't think she can move," I said to Glo. "I think you made her *like* a rock."

"Bummer," Glo said. "What should we do with her? I guess we could still throw her in the ocean."

I looked over at Clara. "We should get Clara to the hospital."

"Get her out of here first," Clara said. "I'm not leaving my bakery unprotected with Nutso here in the front shop."

"Nutso looks to be stuck in one spot," I said to Clara.

"Yes, but the frickberry hasn't come in yet," Glo said. "So this might not last forever."

There was flour everywhere, and I wasn't taking chances with it, so I snapped on rubber gloves and went over the entire room, including Deirdre Early, with the Shop-Vac.

"How are you holding up?" I asked Clara.

"I'm okay. Get me a towel so I don't spew blood everywhere." She looked down at her arm. "My arm is killing me. It feels like I twisted it when I fell."

Glo got a towel for Clara, and I put the Shop-Vac away and rolled the hand truck into the front shop. We loaded Early onto the truck, I rolled her through the kitchen, out the back door, and set her in the parking lot. Aside from not being able to move, she seemed in pretty good shape. She was making low growling sounds and rolling her eyes, but that was about all she could do.

We walked Clara out to Glo's car, I locked the shop, and Glo drove us to the hospital. I called Diesel on the way and told him what had happened.

An hour later, the gash on Clara's forehead was getting sutured together, and her broken arm was in a soft cast.

Diesel was slouched in a chair in the waiting room, paging through a copy of *Sports Illustrated.* He looked up when Glo and I entered from the treatment area. "How is she?"

"She's going to be fine," I said. "She's going to have a major headache for a while, and unfortunately she got a hairline break in her arm when she fell."

"I drove past the parking lot on my way here," Diesel said. "Early was still there, looking like a statue. Maybe you want to put a bagel in her hand and stand her on the sidewalk by Dazzle's front door." He looked at his watch. "How much longer do you think this will take?"

"No more than an hour," I said.

Glo pulled a bunch of magazines out of the rack on the wall. "I can stay with her and take her home. I don't mind waiting. I haven't read any of these."

Diesel and I left the hospital and got on 1A south to Boston.

"Do you think Deirdre Early is Anarchy?" I asked Diesel. "She's flat-out crazy, and she has a horrible temper. She got mad in the bakery, and the bagels were dancing in the display case. She's like Poltergeist Woman."

"I like the thought. It would be a huge

pain if there were *two* crazy, power-hungry women after the stone."

"Plus Wulf."

"Yeah. Don't want to forget Wulf. What did he say to you this morning?"

"You knew I talked to Wulf?"

"I have Wulf radar. Little alarms go off in my brain when he's near. I get a cramp in my ass."

"He was following Anarchy, and I stumbled onto him when I walked out of the house. He said Anarchy has targeted me since she didn't have any luck recruiting Hatchet. That's why I thought Early could be Anarchy. Early said either I was her minion or I was dead."

"We need to move faster through these clues," Diesel said. "There are too many players, and they're holding too much power, and they're all postal."

Forty minutes later, we were on Beacon Hill trying to get to Joy Street. Joy Street was another of those places you can't get to from here in a car. Every street was one way going in the wrong direction. Diesel finally found a parking place on Mt. Vernon, and we walked a block to Joy. We walked the entire length of Joy and ended on the corner of Joy and Beacon.

"I'm not getting anything," Diesel said. "Joy is like any other residential street on the Hill. Expensive homes. Affluent residents. Nothing out of the ordinary for Beacon Hill. I was hoping to find something relating to the 'selfless' part of the riddle . . . like a church."

I had the riddle written on a note card. "Those whose minds are shaped by selfless thoughts give Joy when they speak or act. Joy follows them like a shadow that never leaves them," I said.

It was late afternoon and the sun was low in the sky. Joy Street had been sunny when we arrived, and we were now standing in shade.

"We're in the shadow," I said. "The sun is going down and Joy Street is in shadow. Could this be the shadow of Joy?"

"It could be, but it still doesn't get us anywhere. For the most part, the shadow is coming from the State House. And the shadow keeps changing. The sun moves across the sky and the shadow moves with it. The pinnacle of the dome will point to at least a half dozen addresses by the time the sun sets."

"If the shadow in the second part of the riddle comes from the State House, maybe the first part of the riddle refers to people in public office. *Those whose minds are shaped by selfless thoughts give Joy when they speak.*"

"That's a stretch," Diesel said.

I grabbed him by his hand and pulled him after me. "Come on. Let's look at the State House."

"What's with all the enthusiasm to save the world all of a sudden?"

"I'm motivated. People want to kill me. I figure if I find the stupid stone, I can get on with my life."

"So it's not about the world . . . it's all about you?"

"Yeah. I don't actually care about the world. And I don't always recycle, either. Sometimes I throw my yogurt cups in the garbage."

"Shocking," Diesel said.

He answered his cell phone and stared down at his shoe while he listened. He gave his head a small shake, as if he didn't believe what he was hearing. Or maybe it was that he didn't want to hear what someone was telling him.

"I'm on it," Diesel said. And he disconnected.

"Well?" I asked him.

"Sandman ran away again."

We were across the street from the Boston Common, and Diesel looked out at the park.

"Let's go for a walk," Diesel said.

"You're going to look for Sandman?"

"Yeah."

"What about saving the world?"

"This won't take long."

We crossed the street and took the footpath to the Frog Pond. When the weather turns cold, the Frog Pond is flooded for ice skating. When the weather is warm, the Frog Pond is turned into a wading pool. Today was in between seasons and the Frog Pond was closed. We walked past the Frog Pond to the bandstand and found Sandman sitting on the steps, soaking up the day's last rays of sun.

"Hey, Morty," Diesel said. "How's it going?"

"Not bad," Morty said. "Just living the good life."

"Everyone would feel better if you were living the good life at your son's house."

"My son's a weenie."

"We're going to take a tour of the State House. Why don't you come with us."

"Is it a caper?"

"Yeah."

"What about my baloney sandwich? Will I be back here in time for the food truck?"

"I'll make sure you get a baloney sandwich."

"Okay! I'm in."

We retraced our steps through the park, hiked up Beacon Street, and then we hiked up about a million steps to the front of the State House. We followed signs to the visitors' entrance to the right of the main gate. The door was locked. No one around. The State House was closed to visitors on Sunday.

"No problem," Diesel said.

He moved his hand along the door,

the locks tumbled, and he opened the door.

"This is the State House," I said. "You can't break into the State House!"

"I'm not breaking in," he said. "The door is unlocked."

"Oh boy," Morty said. "This is good. Nothing like a little B&E to get your blood pumping."

We walked in and looked around. Empty.

"There's something going on in here somewhere," Diesel said. "I can hear activity."

I stood very still. "I don't hear anything."

"That's because I'm the one with the heightened senses, and you're the one . . ."

Diesel stopped in mid-sentence.

"And I'm the one who makes cupcakes?"

"Honey, there's nothing wrong with making cupcakes."

"You are so not going to see me naked."

"You haven't seen her naked yet?" Morty said to Diesel. "What's with that?

How long you two been together? Maybe we need one of those man-to-man talks. I would have nailed her by now. I got a way with women. Once they see I can bend a spoon, they're all over me. It's like taking candy from a baby. So, what are we gonna steal this time?"

"We don't know," I told him. "We're scouting."

We walked to the left, past the bookstore, and stopped at the elevators.

"Going up," Diesel said, pushing the button.

I stepped back. "No way. This is as far as I'm going. We can come back tomorrow when the building is open."

"I thought you were motivated."

"I'm not motivated to go to prison!"

The elevator doors opened, and Diesel pushed me in. "You worry about rules too much."

"She reminds me of my son," Morty said. "Uptight fussbudget. I love him, but I'm not gonna lie to myself. He's got problems. And he's not even good-looking, like me. I don't know how he ever found a woman to marry him. I guess it's what they say . . . there's a lid for every pot."

We stepped out of the elevator at the second floor, and it was clear the noise was coming from the back of the building. We walked through the Hall of Flags toward the Great Hall. The glass doors to the Great Hall were open and the hall was being prepared for a party. Round tables seating eight each were set around the perimeter of the room. They were draped in red linen tablecloths and decorated with candles and flowers. Two bars were manned by bartenders in white shirt, black tie, and black slacks. Two carving stations were being prepared by chefs in silly hats and white chef coats. And two long buffet tables were getting stocked with a mountainous shrimp display, too many steaming chafing dishes to take a count, an artistic arrangement of breads, salads, sauces, pickled vegetables, exotic sliced fruit, smelly cheese, and smoked salmon.

"That's some spread," Morty said, "but I don't see no baloney."

A guy in a white chef coat came up to

us. "You look like you're lost. You must be from the agency."

"Yep," I said. "The agency sent us."

"Doors are open in fifteen minutes, and I'm short. You can get changed downstairs. You know the drill, right? You've done this before?"

"Oh yeah," I said. "Lots of times."

He checked Morty out. "He looks kind of old."

"I'm old as dirt," Morty said, "but you should see what I can do with a spoon."

The guy in the chef coat shook his head. "Sky-high unemployment, and this is the best they could send me." And he hurried away.

"Now what?" I said to Diesel.

"We go downstairs and get changed. If we look like waiters, we won't stand out, and we'll have access to the building."

"How do we get downstairs?"

"There's a bunch of fancy-dressed waiters coming from the door over there," Morty said.

Fifteen minutes later, we were dressed in white shirts, black bow ties, and black slacks, and we were back in the Great

Hall. Morty and I looked halfway decent. Diesel looked like a Chippendale's dancer ready to burst out of his clothes.

Men in black tie and women in cocktail dresses were entering, smiling, talking, looking for their tables. The waitstaff was circulating with glasses of champagne and hors d'oeuvres on silver trays.

"When this hall gets filled with people, no one will notice if we leave to do our thing," Diesel said. "Grab a tray and blend in until then."

Morty got a tray of stuffed mushrooms. "Look at this," he said. "Would you take something that looks like this from a stranger and eat it? I got a new rule since my time living in the park. I don't eat food that's brown."

"Don't let him out of your sight," Diesel said to me.

I trailed after Morty. He offered his mushrooms and I offered chicken on a skewer. Neither of us had a lot of takers. People were going directly to the buffet table and taking seats.

"It's like I got cooties," Morty said. "No one wants one of these crapola brown things. Not that I blame them. I feel like I'm serving goose turds. And look at this party. What a bunch of stiffs. There isn't anybody here under eighty. They should be passing out Metamucil shooters. These people are falling asleep, and they're not even talking to me. I bet I could liven it up."

"We don't want it livened up. We're just waiting for a signal from Diesel to sneak out."

"I used to be the life of the party," Morty said. "Did I tell you about the time I bent three spoons at once? I was crafty about it, too. I don't move my lips or anything."

Oh dear God, I thought. Where the heck was Diesel? Five more minutes of Morty, and I was going to be stretched out under a buffet table.

I rearranged my meat on a stick and realized voices were raised two tables down from me. Everyone was focused on one of the women at the table.

"Look at her spoon," someone said. "It bent all by itself."

A collective gasp went up and attention turned to the man next to her.

"It's a miracle!" one of the women said. "Another spoon just bent."

"It's a trick," someone else said. "They must be trick spoons."

I looked over at Morty. His face was red, his eyes were narrowed to slits, and he was sweating.

"I've got one, too," someone yelled.

"Me, too!"

"I'm hot, baby," Morty said. "I'm back! Morty Sandman's still got it. It's a record! No one's ever bent more than four spoons at once. Boy, I feel like a million bucks. I bet I could bend every spoon here."

Diesel appeared out of nowhere and ushered Morty out of the hall.

"What's the rush?" Morty said. "I was just getting started. I was on a roll."

"If you kept bending spoons in there, they'd clear the place out and call in an exorcist."

We kept our trays in case we ran into security, and we walked to the front of the building.

"I did some research while you were serving," Diesel said. "The shadow on Joy Street is for the most part thrown by the dome in the front of the building, so I think we should start by looking at the dome. It sits over the Senate Chamber on the third floor."

We took the elevator to the third floor and Diesel led us into the Senate Chamber. The Chamber walls were painted brick and there were busts of famous people stuck in niches. Above this, on the fourth floor, was gallery seating. And above everything was the dome, decorated in a sort of starburst pattern with an elaborate wrought-iron chandelier hanging from the middle of it.

We walked around the room, reading plaques and examining the sculptures. We looked up at the dome. No frescoes. Very simple artwork.

"There's a cupola on the top of the dome," Diesel said. "There has to be a way to get up there. Usually, there are steps winding up. I've been to the top of lots of domes in Europe. Usually, the steps wind along an interior wall. In this case, what we're seeing must be a false ceiling and not actually the skin of the dome."

I didn't consider this to be good news.

I was a little claustrophobic, and I didn't like heights all that much, either.

We went up to the fourth floor and walked through the gallery areas. We looked down at the Senate seating. We looked up at the dome.

"This is dumb," Morty said. "You don't know what the heck you're even looking for. I could have stayed at the party and bent spoons."

"Jeez Louise," I said. "Will you give us a break with the spoons already?"

"You're getting a little snippy, missy," Morty said. He looked at Diesel. "That's what happens when they don't get enough satisfaction, if you know what I mean."

"Hey, I'm doing my best," Diesel said, "but she has issues."

"I *do not* have issues," I said. "You're the one with the issues. You're the one who has to save the world. Am I all that hot on saving the world? No, but I'm being a good sport about it. You could at least recognize that. You could say, *Wow, Lizzy, thanks for helping me out*."

"Maybe it's that time of the month," Morty said.

"Hold me back," I said to Diesel. "I'm going to kill him."

"What else?" Diesel asked me.

"What do you mean?"

"What else is bothering you?"

"I don't want to go up in the dome."

"Now we're getting somewhere," Diesel said.

"So I don't have to go up?"

"Yeah, you still have to go up, but you can whimper like a little girl if you want."

I left the gallery and walked the hall that ran around the outside of the room. There were windows looking out on Boston, and between the windows were murals. Some of the murals were of farm scenes. Some were military, showing battles of the Revolution. Some were of statesmen. They all had appropriate quotes written in fancy script worked into the art. I stopped to look at a mural depicting a farm scene, and the quote took my breath away. *Sometimes too hot the eye of heaven shines.*

Holy cow. It was the line from Reedy's Shakespeare anthology.

CHAPTER EIGHTEEN

I peered out the window that was next to the Shakespeare quote, and I looked down on Joy Street. Diesel walked over and stood next to me.

"Boston looks nice from up here," he said. "This is my favorite American city."

"I'm surprised you don't live here. Why did you choose to live in Marblehead?"

"I had to be near you."

It was the second time in the last two minutes I went breathless. When I get up in the morning, I try not to focus on the possibility that I'm one of two people on this earth with the ability to recognize an object that might make everyone's life a misery. Truth is, a lot of the time when I'm tagging along with Diesel I'm feeling like Alice when she fell down the rabbit hole—that I'm in an insanely weird dream, and I'll wake up at any moment and everything will be normal again.

And then there are times like this, when I'm reminded that I've been assigned a protector, and the magnitude of my responsibility sinks in.

"I found the clue," I said to Diesel. "It's painted into this mural."

He draped an arm around me and read the quote attributed to Shakespeare. "Good job. There's a sun in it, too. The hot eye of heaven. And it's shining down on the farmer's fields."

"This mural is a mosaic," Marty said, leaning close to the mural, examining the surface. "Inside the sun is a piece of tile shaped like a key."

Diesel took the Lovey key out of his pocket and placed it over the mosaic key. It was a perfect fit, and a number appeared in the farmhouse. The number was followed by a capital *J*.

"This could all be a colossal nineteenth-century joke," I said. "An endless scavenger hunt that goes nowhere."

I heard the elevator doors open, and a security guard walked our way.

"No one is supposed to be in this part of the building," he said.

"Sorry," I said. "We didn't realize. We had a free moment and I guess we got carried away. We've never been in the State House before, and it's really interesting."

"If you come back during the week, you can take a tour," the guard said. "I'm going to have to ask you to go back to the Great Hall now."

"We should be getting back anyway," I said. "Our break time is over."

Diesel pocketed the key. We took the elevator to the second floor and went back to the reception. The guests were still seated. Chamber music could faintly be heard over the crush of conversation.

"Watch this," Morty said. "I could do it with my eyes closed."

A cheer went up from across the room.

"I got one!" someone yelled.

"Am I good or what?" Morty said.

We went down to the employee locker room, changed back into our own clothes, and left through a door that led to Hancock Street. We walked Hancock to Mt. Vernon, and Mt. Vernon to Joy. The house number that appeared on the mosaic was on the first block between Beacon and Mt. Vernon. We stood on the sidewalk and stared at the redbrick town house. Four floors, plus a garden level. Not in terrible condition, but not newly renovated, either.

There weren't any lights on in the house. Either no one was home, or else someone went to bed early. It was too dark to read the bronze plaque by the door.

"It must be a historic house," Morty said. "They always have plaques on them like that."

Curiosity got the better of me, and I crept up the steps to the small front stoop to better see the writing on the plaque.

"It says this is a historic house designed by William Butterfield in 1880," I whispered. "Its name is The Key House, after its first occupant, Malcom Key."

I touched the plaque with my fingertip and felt the trapped energy. "It's the plaque," I said, motioning Diesel to come take a look. "I can feel the energy."

Diesel examined the plaque and felt around the edges. "I can't just remove it," he said. "It's cemented into the brick."

"I'm hungry," Morty said. "I had some of them hors d'oeuvres, but I never got my baloney sandwich."

Diesel looked at his watch. "I'm supposed to hand you over to your son in a half hour. Let's go back to the car, and I'll figure this out later."

We walked to the car, and Diesel drove to Beacon and double-parked in front of a small grocery store. I ran in and got Morty a loaf of worthless white bread, half a pound of baloney, and a bag of chips, and I was back before the police spotted our illegally parked car.

Diesel skirted the Public Garden and pulled in behind the Four Seasons Hotel. Morty's son was already there.

"He's not so bad," Morty said. "I'm sort of looking forward to going home. I got a nice television in my room, and I got my baloney."

We handed Morty off, and Diesel got back into the stream of traffic, driving away from Beacon Hill.

"Where are we going?" I asked him.

"As long as we're here, I thought I'd check on Deirdre Early. There are a few things I'd like to talk to her about."

"Such as?"

"Hitting people in the head, threatening you, Anarchy."

"All good topics of conversation," I said. "Maybe you want to take five or six Advil before knocking on her door."

Diesel turned onto Commonwealth Avenue, and we immediately saw the fire trucks a block away, parked in front of Early's house. He pulled in behind one of the trucks, and we sat there for a moment looking at the disaster in front of us. Early's house appeared to be gutted. Windows were blown out. The exterior was soot-stained. The roof was partially collapsed.

"I warned her she was going to self-combust," I said to Diesel.

His smile was grim. "That would be the hoped-for scenario."

We left the car and joined two of the firefighters, relaxing by their truck, sipping coffee.

"What happened?" Diesel asked.

"Not sure," one of the guys said. "Probably some accelerant involved, since it went through the house like lightning. Impossible to know for sure, but it doesn't look like anyone was home. Lucky we got here fast and kept it from spreading."

I was thinking probably when the roof went it released all the evil spirits into the air, like the scene in *Ghostbusters* when the spook containment facility exploded.

Twenty minutes later, we were standing in front of The Key House again, and Diesel had a big screwdriver in his hand.

"So you think that screwdriver is going to do the job?" I asked him.

"I shouldn't have a problem if it's just cemented in at the corners."

"And if the whole thing is cemented?"

"I'll have a problem. Keep your eye out for company."

He rammed the screwdriver into the brick and mortar, chipping away chunks of brick.

"You're making a mess," I said.

He stopped work and looked at me. "Do you want to try this?"

"No."

Thunk, thunk, thunk.

"Jeez," I said. "That's awfully loud."

"I'm starting to think I'd be better off with Hatchet," Diesel said. "At least I could beat him."

"Just trying to be helpful," I said. "I thought you'd want to know you were loud."

Second-floor lights went on in The Key House.

"Uh-oh," I said. "Can you hurry it up?"

Diesel rammed the screwdriver in one last time, wrenched it back, and the plaque popped off. He scooped it up and stepped off the stoop just as the front door opened and a man wearing boxers and a striped pajama top looked out at us.

"What the devil?" the man said.

We turned and ran, and I heard the man whistle and yell for Bruno. Seconds later, Bruno bounded out of The Key House and took off after us.

"Dog," I said, gasping for air. *"BIG DOG!"*

The dog was doing a lot better on four legs than I was doing on my two. We were still a block from the car, and Bruno was gaining. Diesel stopped in front of a house with a six-foot privacy fence, grabbed me, and threw me over.

One minute, I was running for all I was worth, and next thing, I was flying through the air, and then—*wump*—I was flat on my back in someone's backyard. Diesel followed me over, landing on his feet.

He bent down and looked at me. "Are you okay?"

"Unh."

Bruno was barking and scratching at the fence.

"He's going to bring people," Diesel said, pulling me to my feet. "We have to go."

We looked around. No place to go. Six-foot fence on all sides. No gates.

"I'm going to alley-oop you into the next yard," Diesel said.

"No!"

Too late. I was over the fence. Diesel came next. Same deal. No way out.

"This is ridiculous," Diesel said.

He opened the back door to the house and the alarm went off. We raced through, found the front door, and walked out of the house.

"That was easy," he said.

Diesel took the 1A all the way into Salem and drove to the bakery. I'd called to check on Clara and found she was at her sister's house for the night. Glo was off on a date with the bellringer, and no one knew if Deirdre Early was still in the parking lot.

"What are we going to do if she's still there?" I asked Diesel.

"We're going to ignore her, break into the bakery, and get something to eat. I'm starving."

He turned the corner, his headlights flashed on the lot, and the lot appeared to be empty, with the exception of a grotesque, twisted, large black piece of metal.

"What is that?" I asked.

"I think it's your car," Diesel said.

"It can't possibly be my car."

Diesel parked, we got out, and looked at the charred mess.

"I'm pretty sure it's your car," Diesel said. "I can see part of the license plate."

"I loved that car!"

"No you didn't," Diesel said. "It was one step away from scrap metal."

"Yes, but now I have *no* scrap metal."

"Let's think about what we have here," Diesel said. "Someone torched your car and Early's town house. Probably the same person. Possibly Early, although I don't know why she'd burn down her own house."

"Because she's insane?"

"Yeah, that could be one possibility."

"And then we also have a *missing* Early. Which could be that either the spell didn't stick or else someone stole her."

"I'm going with the spell didn't stick. I can't imagine anyone wanting Deirdre Early."

"Bottom line is I have no idea what the hell's going on," Diesel said. "Are we raiding the bakery or do you have something better to eat at your house?"

"I doubt there's anything left here. We mostly do doughnuts and cookies on Sunday, and Clara isn't opening for business tomorrow."

CHAPTER NINETEEN

Cat was waiting for us when we walked into the house. I scratched him behind his ear and apologized for leaving him alone all day. I think he might have rolled his eyes at me, but it's hard to tell, since he only has one that works. I gave him a can of cat food and pulled stuff out of the refrigerator for a frittata.

I'd had a chance to look at the plaque on the way home. There were some markings on the back that looked like hieroglyphics and random letters. I could feel a little heat and a mild vibration, but nothing to make my hair curl.

Diesel was in the living room with the plaque and my computer, and I could hear the television droning in the background. Undoubtedly some sort of sporting event.

I brought him a beer and some cheese and crackers to hold him until the frittata was out of the oven. "How's it going? Any ideas?"

"The original owner of The Key House, Malcom Key, and the architect, William M. Butterfield, belonged to the Boston Society of Natural History. They would have known Monroe Tichy, and most likely one or both of them was a follower of Lovey, or at least knew him. So maybe the Society is the common denominator. I'm guessing Duane and an early owner of the Van Gogh painting were also Society members."

"And either Lovey or one of the Society members had the unique ability to energize an object in such a way that another kind of energy would trigger a message."

"Yup."

"Do you know where any of this takes us next?"

"No. It would help if something magically appeared on the plaque."

We looked at the plaque but nothing appeared.

"It's always something different," I said. "The first clue was visible to Glo. The second clue was produced by the tone of the bell. The third clue responded to Carl. And the fourth clue was produced by the key."

"I have no basis for thinking this, but I can't shake the feeling that the writing on the back of the plaque is the clue."

I left Diesel to study the clue he'd copied onto paper and returned to the kitchen. I didn't have fresh greens for a salad, but I had some frozen French bread I could defrost, and there were vegetables in the frittata.

The towels and sheets were still on the windows, and not doing a lot for my decorating scheme or my mood.

"Someone toasted my car," I said to Cat. "I think it might have been Deirdre Early. She's a really mean person."

I took the frittata out of the oven, gave a slice to Cat, and plated the rest for Diesel and me, along with the bread. I brought the food into the living room and we ate in front of the television.

"I found a connection," Diesel said. "In 1885, a secret society, Sphinx, was founded at Dartmouth College. In 1903, the society erected a Sphinx Tomb on a small piece of land on Wheelock Street on the Dartmouth campus. William M. Butterfield was the architect for the Tomb. I downloaded a picture of it, and it's hard to be sure, because the resolution isn't as sharp as I'd like, but I think there are markings on the Sphinx cornerstone that resemble the hieroglyphics on the back of the plaque."

I looked at the downloaded picture and gave an inadvertent shudder. "Whoa, this is solemn. It actually looks like a tomb."

It was a windowless gray stone structure with stone steps leading up to a large solid door that was bordered by columns reminiscent of Egyptian temples. Difficult to tell how large the building was from the photo.

"Does this mean we'll be going to Dartmouth?" I asked.

"It's the best lead I have so far."

"Are we going tonight?"

"No. You have to get naked tonight."

"In your dreams."

"Frequently," Diesel said. "You look good." He stared down at his empty plate. "Is there dessert?"

"Fruit."

"Fruit isn't a dessert unless it's in pie crust."

I had my cell phone clipped to my jeans waistband, and I felt it buzz. I looked at the readout and saw Glo's number.

"Hey," I said. "What's going on?"

"He wants the Lovey key," Glo said.

"Who?"

"Wulf. He has me, Lizzy. I don't know where I am. It's dark and it smells like dirt, and Hatchet is here and he has knives. And he cut me, and I'm bleeding."

Her voice was shaking, and I could hear she was crying.

"How bad are you bleeding?"

"Not bad, but it hurts. And he says he'll cut me more if you don't bring the key."

"Is Wulf there?"

"He was, but he left. And now I'm alone with Hatchet."

"Where are we supposed to bring the key?"

"Hatchet is going to text you the address."

She sucked in a sob, and the connection was broken.

I felt all the blood leave my brain, and bells started to clang in my head. I felt Diesel's hand at the back of my neck, pushing my head down between my knees.

"Breathe," Diesel said.

I got it together and sat up. "Sorry, that was a horrible phone call. They have Glo, and they want the key."

"Is it a serious threat?"

"It sounded serious. She was crying, and she said Hatchet cut her." I watched my phone for a text message. "He's going to text me the address for the drop."

Diesel had his hand on my shoulder. "She'll be fine. We'll do whatever we have to to get her back." He was quiet for a moment, lost in thought. "It's interesting that they want the key," Diesel said. "We used the key to get the clue in the State House. It didn't occur to me that the key might have another purpose."

"Maybe they're two steps behind us."

Diesel shook his head. "I think Wulf has always been two steps ahead of us. He's using Hatchet as a dupe to slow us down."

"Do you think Hatchet knows he's a dupe?"

Diesel shrugged. "Hatchet sees his job as serving his liege lord in whatever capacity. His role is to do or die and not question why."

"Jeez."

"Yeah," Diesel said. "You'd suck at it."

My phone chirped and the address came up in my text messages.

"I've got it," I said. "They want the key brought to Carter Street in Salem, and they'll swap the key for Glo."

Diesel was on his feet. "Let's go."

We locked the house, and in minutes we were leaving Marblehead and crossing into Salem. I was trying to stay calm, but I was shaking from anger and adrenaline. And I was heartsick. I was supposed to be saving the world, but my two best friends were hurt because of me.

Carter Street was in a residential part of North Salem. Most of the houses had been converted to multifamily or apartments and were in various stages of renovation, some showing obvious effects of a bad economy. I counted off numbers and had Diesel stop at a gray Georgian Colonial. Even at night I could see that paint was peeling from window frames and the roof was in disrepair. There were no lights shining from windows. The houses on either side were dark as well.

"Wulf's here," Diesel said. "His car is parked in the driveway."

We walked to the door and Hatchet opened it just as Diesel was about to knock. Hatchet stepped back, and I could sense Wulf more than see him. He was lost in the dark room, with only his pale face visible.

"I want to see her," Diesel said.

"The emotional drama isn't necessary," Wulf said. "This is a simple transaction."

He snapped his fingers at Hatchet,

and Hatchet scurried into another room and returned with Glo. Glo looked disheveled and disoriented, and she had a bandage on her forearm.

"I'm afraid Hatchet got carried away in my absence," Wulf said. "Nothing serious, but she might drool a little for an hour or two."

Diesel gave Wulf the key, and Wulf motioned for Hatchet to release Glo.

"You would make a terrible general," Wulf said to Diesel. "You're willing to sacrifice the many for the one."

"I was under the impression the key had already served its purpose."

"It's *the key,*" Wulf said. "It's the last step in the process."

"How do you know?"

"It was all in the little book. While you were out bumbling around searching for clues, I was studying Lovey's sonnets. And I finally have the last piece of the riddle."

"Why did you have Hatchet following us, trying to get the key and the clues, if it was all in the book?" I asked him.

"There was no guarantee that the book would give me the final clue. Lovey was a complicated, devious man. So while I was working my way through his obscure references, I directed Hatchet to ensure you didn't succeed in your treasure hunt."

"What did you give Glo?" I asked. "She looks drugged."

"Hatchet was showing her his prowess with a knife and he sliced a little deep," Wulf said. "He gave her an herb to stop the bleeding, but it has some side effects. She should be fine in a few minutes. Hatchet acts the fool, but he's one of the world's leading experts on medieval torture and toxins."

"Thank you, sire," Hatchet said.

We led Glo out to the car and buckled her in.

"Are you okay?" I asked her.

"Peaches," she said. And she drooled on her shirt.

We stopped at Diesel's apartment, got Carl, and put him in the backseat with Glo.

"Eeh?" he said to Glo.

Glo nodded her head like a bobblehead doll. "Pigeon."

"Maybe we should take her to the

clinic and get her checked out," I said to Diesel.

Diesel drove to the clinic, but by the time we got there, Glo was coming around.

"That was f-f-f-freaking scary," Glo said, her teeth chattering. "Hatchet is nuts!"

"Do you want a doctor to look at your cut?" I asked her. "Do you think you need stitches?"

"No. I want to go home. I want to take a shower. I can't get the smell of dirt out of my nose."

"They must have had you in a cellar with a dirt floor," I said.

"Maybe, but I think the smell was coming from Hatchet. I don't think there's any electricity in that house. It was dark, except for a lantern-type flashlight Hatchet used to show me his knives. He had them all laid out on a table. Some had curved blades, and some had wavy blades, and they were all different sizes, and they were all razor sharp. He said he's been collecting knives since he was seven years old. And he had a suitcase like traveling salesmen use, and it was filled with powders and potions you could use to poison someone. And he had poisonous spiders in jars and vials of snake venom.

"It might have been cool to see all that stuff if I wasn't handcuffed. I always thought it would be fun to be handcuffed in certain situations, but turns out it isn't fun to be handcuffed in *any* situation. It's scary, scary, scary. Especially when someone picks out a knife and deliberately cuts you with it. And after I talked to you, he wanted to try out another knife and make another cut, but Wulf walked in."

"Wulf stopped him."

"Yeah. Wulf got real mad. And let me tell you, when Wulf gets mad, you're afraid to even breathe. I could see him from the light of the lantern, and he didn't have any expression on his face, except his eyes were black and hard, like black glass. And when he spoke, his voice was soft, but every word was clear and precise, like he knew he was talking to an idiot. And I got the feeling if the idiot didn't do the right thing, he could be drinking the snake venom."

"Did Wulf say anything about the Luxuria Stone?" Diesel asked Glo.

"No. He doesn't talk much. He asked Hatchet if I made the call. He looked at my arm to see if I needed stitches and decided it wasn't necessary. Then he told Hatchet to clean it and bandage it. And when Wulf was near me, he smelled like Sambuca. Totally terrifying and at the same time I had this crazy desire to lick him."

"I've noticed that same scent," I said. "Whenever Wulf is near, I always catch a faint hint of anise. You always smell like Christmas," I said to Diesel. "You smell like butter cookies, fir trees, and cloves."

"It's a curse," Diesel said. "Women and small children follow me around."

Glo looked out the window. "This is your street," she said to me.

"I thought you'd be more comfortable spending the night here with us."

"Thanks. That would be great. I'm still pretty freaked out. I never even saw Hatchet coming. I parked my car, and I was walking to my apartment, and all of a sudden he grabbed me. I guess he used a stun gun on me, because in an instant I was on the ground. Next thing I knew, I was handcuffed and there was something over my head so I couldn't see. I'm surprised I didn't have a stroke or a heart attack, because my heart was pounding like it was going to jump out of my chest. I had no idea who kidnapped me or where we were going. And then there was the dirt smell. When you're handcuffed and have a bag over your head, dirt smells like death. I was sort of relieved when I found out it was Hatchet, until he insisted on doing knife demonstrations."

Diesel pulled to the curb and cut the engine. We all got out and Diesel stopped us at the door.

"Someone's been here," he said, opening the door, going in first. "I locked the door when we left, and it wasn't locked just now."

I followed him in and my first thought was of Cat. Everything I owned could be stolen or destroyed as long as Cat was okay. Diesel flipped the light on, and I looked down and saw drops of blood on the floor. My breath caught in my chest for a beat, until Cat strolled in from the kitchen. I scooped Cat up and inspected him, relieved that he wasn't bleeding.

"The plaque is gone," Diesel said. "It was on the coffee table. Check on the other empowered objects to see if they've been stolen as well."

I went to the laundry, and then I ran upstairs and looked under my bed. Diesel and Glo were in the kitchen when I came down.

"Everything else is here," I said.

Diesel was at the cookie jar. "Someone broke one of the windowpanes and unlocked the back door."

"So we know it wasn't Hatchet, because he was with Glo. And we know it wasn't Wulf, because, like you, he can unlock doors."

"Yeah," Diesel said. "That leaves Deirdre Early. I should have known the instant I stepped in and smelled smoke."

"And the blood on the floor . . ." I said.

We all turned to Cat, who was sitting, calmly grooming. Ninja Cat strikes again.

"He deserves a steak dinner," Diesel said.

Cat looked over at him and blinked. And I'm pretty sure Cat was smiling.

I sent Glo and Carl into the living room with the cookie jar, and put Glo in charge of the channel changer. I scrubbed the blood off the floor, and Diesel tacked a board over the broken window.

"We need to get an early start for Dartmouth tomorrow," Diesel said. "Fortunately, you have the day off. Maybe Glo will stay here with Carl."

CHAPTER TWENTY

Diesel's idea of an early start is sometime before noon. I made French toast and a gallon of coffee for everyone, and asked Clara if she would please retrieve my license plate when she returned to the bakery. I'd deal with the rest of the car carcass when I got back. I expected that would be sometime before dark. I had no idea what we'd find when we got to the Sphinx, but I couldn't imagine there would be much left. I was sure Wulf had a good head start on us.

It takes about two and a half hours to drive to Hanover, New Hampshire. The beginning of the trip is almost as enjoyable as the drive to Boston. Which is to say, it sucks. Little towns, lots of traffic, annoying ways to get lost. Once you hit Route 89, it all changes, and the closer you get to Hanover, the more jaw-droppingly beautiful it becomes. Forested foothill mountains with granite cliffs and long vistas, an occasional marshy bog, beautifully maintained roads with little traffic.

We took Route 91 from 89, got off at the exit for Norwich, Vermont, crossed the Connecticut River, and rolled into Hanover. The first impression is that this is a movie set for a small Ivy League, New England college town. Autumn was in the air and leaves were dropping from trees. Students were everywhere in hooded sweatshirts, jeans, and trail shoes. Everyone looked healthy, and you could imagine them eating sprouted wheat bread and drinking lots of stale beer out of plastic party cups.

The college was to the left, with domes and spires and classroom buildings that date back as far as the late 1700s and early 1800s.

Main Street, with shops and pubs, shot off to the right. It was lined with redbrick buildings, benches and trees, and parking meters.

The Hanover Inn occupied the corner of Main and East Wheelock. It's a big, blocky, redbrick structure with rocking chairs on its wide porch. And opposite the Inn is the Dartmouth Green.

We were on East Wheelock Street, and there were dorms to the left and right of me. I was thinking this was incredibly appealing, and maybe I would want to live here some day. Open a bakery of my own and make healthy treats and homemade granola for the college faculty. And then I saw the Sphinx, and I had second thoughts about Hanover.

The building was a temple, a tomb, a forbidding gray stone bunker. It could have been a bomb shelter. It was nicely proportioned but cold and unwelcoming. And it looked forgotten, sitting forlorn in a scraggly copse of undernourished trees, perched on hardscrabble grass without a single azalea bush to soften its appearance. A hundred years ago, it had no doubt been the pride of a secret society when secret societies flourished. But that time had come and gone, and the Sphinx now looked like a beautifully designed but lone monument in an unattended boneyard.

Diesel found parking a block away, and we walked back to take a closer look. No sign of Wulf or Hatchet. No sign of Deirdre Early. No sign that anyone ever used the building. The heavy wood door looked completely unused. Diesel ran his hand over it and wasn't able to find a lock he could open. There was no give when he pushed against it.

We circled the building and found a simple, unassuming door on the east side. It had a five-button security lock that had been pretty well bashed in and what appeared to be the tip of a sword wedged between door and jamb.

"Looks like Hatchet's been here," Diesel said.

"Can you open it?"

He put his hand to it. "It's jammed."

We circled the building several times but couldn't find a way to get in. I had the scrap of paper with the hieroglyphics and scrambled letters on it. We compared the hieroglyphics on my paper to the markings on the tomb's cornerstone and they were exactly the same.

"Do you get any vibes when you touch the building?" Diesel asked me.

I put my hand to the stone. "Nope. Nothing."

I heard sirens and I turned to see a police car race down Wheelock, moving toward Main Street. It was followed by a fire truck and another police car. We left the Sphinx and went to the sidewalk. It was impossible to see exactly what was going on, but smoke billowed into the sky from somewhere on campus.

Diesel and I walked toward the smoke and saw that it was coming from a building on the far side of the Green. We crossed the Green and joined the crowd of students watching the building burn.

I was standing next to a guy with a two-day beard and hair that was in worse shape than Diesel's.

"What building is this?" I asked him. "How did the fire start?"

"This is Parkhurst," he said. "It's an admin building. The Office of Student

Life is in here. Don't know how the fire started."

An older woman who looked like she might work in the building leaned toward us. "I was told some crazy woman came in demanding a list of Sphinx members. And when she didn't get it, she torched the office and ran away."

"The gang's all here," Diesel said to me.

"Now what?" I asked him.

"Lunch," Diesel said. "I'm starving."

We crossed Wheelock, bypassed The Hanover Inn, thinking it looked too classy for us, and settled on Lou's. My rule of thumb is always go with the diner that has a pastry counter right up front. Especially if the pastries are homemade and look like the ones in Lou's case.

There was counter seating and booth seating and we were able to take our pick, since everyone else in town was gawking at the fire. I ordered a burger, and Diesel ordered something called The Big Green, which it turned out meant they emptied the kitchen onto as many plates as it took and tried to cram them onto the small booth table. It was the equivalent of ordering half a cow at Fat Bubba's Steak House. Eggs, pancakes with real maple syrup, bacon, hash browns, sausage, English muffin, and whatever else was buried under the eggs and potatoes.

Diesel shoveled it all in and got a maple-glazed cruller on the way out.

"Impressive," I said to him.

"The food?"

"That, too."

We walked back to the Sphinx and stared at it.

"I've got nothing," I said to Diesel.

"It bothers me that Hatchet and Fire Woman are here, and we're not seeing them."

"Are we talking about Deirdre Early or Anarchy?"

"I'm counting on them being the same person."

"Works for me. We haven't seen Wulf, either."

"I'm sure he's here, somewhere. He's probably napping in his Batmobile, waiting for the moon to come out."

"You don't like him."

"There was a time when I admired

and envied him. His skills came earlier than mine. But we made different life choices, and it's placed us in an adversarial position."

There were some guys and dogs playing with Frisbees on the lawn of a neighboring fraternity.

"Is that Alpha Delta?" I asked Diesel.

"Yeah. It's the fraternity that inspired *Animal House*."

"It's also mentioned in a lot of references as having a secret tunnel to the Sphinx."

Diesel looked at the Sphinx, and he looked at the frat house. He shrugged and set out across the grass. "We've run down every other ridiculous idea, and some of them got us to this point. We might as well run down *this* ridiculous idea, too."

"No stone unturned," I said, jogging to keep up with him.

He went straight to the front door and walked in, with me trailing behind. Two guys turned to look at us.

"Is Scott here?" Diesel asked.

"Yeah, somewhere."

"I'll find him," Diesel said. "Thanks."

And he walked toward the back of the house and down a staircase.

"How do you know where to go?" I asked Diesel.

"They're all the same," Diesel said. "There's always a guy named Scott, and there's always a downstairs party room. And if there's a tunnel, it's not going to originate on the second floor."

The downstairs party room was deserted at this time of the day. The light was dim and the room smelled like beer and salami. It had a bar at one end. Some leather couches. Photographs, banners, plaques, and paddles hung on the walls.

I opened a door to a utility closet and found a trapdoor in the floor. "Trapdoor," I said to Diesel.

Diesel poked his head in and looked down at the door. "Shows promise."

There were flashlights on a shelf in the utility closet. We each took one, closed the door to the closet, eased ourselves through the trapdoor, and descended into the cramped, dark subcellar. Copper water pipes and electrical cables snaked overhead, the floor was dirt, and a metal box sat in a far corner. *Danger—High Voltage* was written on the box, but the box didn't look like it connected to anything. Diesel pushed the box aside and uncovered a wooden hatch. He opened the hatch and flashed some light into it. There was a ladder going down about ten feet to another dirt floor.

I wasn't feeling wonderful about where I was at present, and I *really* didn't want to go down to another level.

"How about if I go back to the closet and stand guard," I said to Diesel. "And you can push on."

"Not necessary," Diesel said. "No one knows we're down here."

"Did I ever mention my slight claustrophobia?"

"Yes. Did I ever mention my *face your fears* philosophy?" Diesel slipped into the opening and dropped out of sight. "There's more headroom here," he called up. "And it looks safe."

I'd broken into a sweat, and my brain was screaming, *Air! Get me fresh air!* I turned toward the stairs that would take me back to the closet, Diesel's hand wrapped around my ankle, and next thing, I was halfway down the ladder. His hands were at my waist, and I was the rest of the way down.

"It's going to be okay," he said. "You're with me. I'm not going to let anything bad happen to you."

"I don't want you to get too offended by this, but that's not doing it for me. I'm having a panic attack. I can't breathe. I'm suffocating. It's too much dirt. There's dirt everywhere."

He pulled me flat against him, and he kissed me. His lips were soft, and his tongue touched mine, and I felt heat move through me. His arms wrapped around me, pressing me into him, the kiss deepened, and when he broke from the kiss, I wasn't thinking about being buried alive under the Alpha Delta house anymore. I was thinking I wanted more kisses. A lot more. In fact, I wouldn't mind if he put his hand on my breast. I wouldn't even mind if he slipped his hand inside my . . .

"Are you okay?" he asked.

"What?"

"Do you still feel panicky?"

"You kissed me because I was having a panic attack?"

"Yeah. Did it work?"

I kicked him hard in the shin.

"Are you sure it's not that time of the month?" Diesel asked.

I smacked the heel of my hand against my forehead. "Unh! Men."

He grabbed my wrist and tugged me along a narrow tunnel. At least, I'm pretty sure it was narrow, because I had my eyes closed, but every now and then my arm brushed against the side. After what seemed like an hour but might have been minutes, Diesel stopped and I could sense the flashlight on me.

"You can open your eyes now," he said. "We're at the end of the tunnel. We're going up."

Praise the Lord.

Diesel climbed the ladder first. He shoved the overhead door open, and light flooded into the tunnel. I was so relieved, I almost burst into tears. I scrambled up the ladder after him and found myself inside what had to be the Sphinx. I'm not sure exactly what I'd expected, but it wasn't what I found. I'd hoped it would be like Cleopatra's barge, but it looked more like the Alpha Delta taproom.

One of the walls contained a fresco depicting St. Peter holding the keys to heaven. Odd for an Egyptian-themed temple, and in direct contrast to the opposing wall, which featured a poster of Jane Fonda as Barbarella.

"I like this fresco," I said to Diesel. "It doesn't completely belong in the room, but it's very handsome." I ran my hand across it and felt the energy. "And it's empowered."

Diesel moved next to me. "Can you isolate the part that's empowered?"

I traced the fresco with my fingertip. "It's the key." I looked more closely. The Lovey Key was embedded into the fresco.

Diesel saw it, too. "Obviously, Wulf or Hatchet has passed through here, and the key must have attached itself on contact."

I scanned the room. "How did they get in? You couldn't open either door."

"They probably came the same way we did."

"A chubby guy in full Renaissance regalia and a man who looks like a vampire just walk into a frat house and let themselves into the dungeon under the taproom?"

"It's a fraternity. You'd be surprised how often that happens. I know. I belonged to a fraternity." He pressed the key and—*whoosh*—part of the wall swung out. "Damn," Diesel said. "Am I good, or what? This is a secret door."

The door opened onto a narrow winding staircase positioned between the outside wall and the inside wall. I followed Diesel into the staircase, and when we were halfway down, the door closed with a click. I retraced my steps and pushed on the door, but it wouldn't open. I couldn't find a handle, a switch, a button. No way to open the door.

"We're locked in," I said to Diesel.

"That's kind of a bummer, because there's no way out down here, and I have no bars on my cell phone."

I joined Diesel at the bottom of the stairs and flicked my flashlight around the room. We were in a sort of grotto.

Stone walls, moldy ceiling, a dark, seemingly endless pool of water.

"How did it come to this?" I asked Diesel. "Everything was going right for me. I had a little house, a job I liked, even a cat. And then you came along, and now I'm going to die."

"We might not die," Diesel said.

"How so?"

Diesel had his flashlight trained to writing on the wall. *Love is a leap of faith*.

"I hate these messages," I said. "I hate them, hate them, hate them! I don't want to see another message for the entire rest of my life."

There was a moment of mutual silence where I suspect we were thinking the same thing . . . that the rest of our lives could be ten or fifteen minutes, depending on how fast the air got used up in here.

"Sorry," I said. "I didn't mean to pitch a fit."

"It's okay. I'm not overjoyed to see more messages, either." He handed me his flashlight. "Hang on to this until I get back."

"Where are you going?"

"I'm taking a leap of faith."

And he jumped into the black water and disappeared.

"No!" I yelled. "Diesel!"

CHAPTER TWENTY-ONE

I had a white-knuckle grip on the flashlight, scanning the water's surface. A minute passed. Two minutes. I was pacing the pool's edge, looking for a sign that Diesel was moving around. A tear trickled down my cheek, and I bit my lip to keep from sobbing.

"If anyone's listening," I whispered, "please don't let him drown."

I thought I saw a ripple, and then Diesel popped his head out in an explosion of water. He swam to the side and hoisted himself out.

"There's an underwater tunnel about

ten feet down," he said. "The tunnel itself isn't real long. Maybe twenty feet. It opens into another grotto. And there's a passage going out of that grotto. I didn't get to explore the passage. You're going to have to leave the flashlight here. It's not waterproof. It'll be useless on the other side."

"I don't know if I can hold my breath long enough."

"You absolutely can. It's not that far. I know exactly where the tunnel starts. We're going to swim over to it, and I'm going to guide you in and push you from behind. Don't kick. Just let me push."

"Oh boy."

"It's not so bad. It's like Indiana Jones. Remember how that big boulder was coming at him in *Raiders of the Lost Ark*? This is a snap compared to that."

I eased myself into the water with Diesel supporting me.

"It's cold," I said.

"Only at first. You'll get used to it."

We scooted around the edge of the pool until Diesel said we were above the start to the tunnel.

I held my breath, and Diesel pulled

me down and pushed my head into the opening. I put my arms out straight, and Diesel propelled us through the passage and kicked us up to the surface.

We climbed out and stood there, dripping wet and taking deep breaths. It was pitch-black, and I couldn't see anything.

"Can you see in the dark?" I asked him.

"Yes. Can you?"

"No. Not even a little."

"Hang on to me, and I'll get us out of here."

The passage was high enough that I didn't have to stoop, and wide enough that my shoulders weren't constantly hitting the sides. My shoes were squishing water, but it was better than walking barefoot. We made a turn, and I saw light ahead. A few more steps and the light was brighter. We took another turn and stepped into a large, domed room. And Hatchet was there. He was sitting on the floor with a lump and a gash on his forehead, looking damp and dejected, surrounded by rats.

I felt myself go rigid with anger, and I

glared at Hatchet. "You sick son of a . . ."

Diesel wrapped an arm around me and walked me back into the passage a couple feet.

"Go easy," Diesel said. "We need him to talk to us."

"He hurt Glo."

"I know, but we want him to tell us things."

I nodded.

"Can you hold it together?"

"Yeah."

"Are you sure?"

"Pretty sure."

We returned to the domed room.

"Hey, how's it going?" Diesel said.

"We shall all die together in this hell-hole, this stinking pit of misery," Hatchet said.

"What's with the rats?"

"They doth like me."

We were on the far side of the room from Hatchet, and I wasn't going any closer. Maybe if Hatchet was Pied Piper to hamsters I could manage, but these rats were as big as barn cats.

"Is that one of your special talents?" I asked Hatchet. "You attract vermin?"

"Apparently. They followed me here from one of the tunnels."

There were four tunnel entrances in the room, plus the tunnel we just left. I tipped my head back and saw that the light was coming from a crack in the domed ceiling high overhead and reflecting off what looked like quartz crystals embedded in the walls of the cave.

"Have you tried all the tunnels?" Diesel asked.

"Yes. 'Tis a maze. I always return to this room. Some are booby-trapped. None are lit. And I cannot see in the dark."

"Is there more water?" I asked him.

"Nay. None that I have found. Just the way we came."

"And you came from Alpha Delta?"

"I did not. My sire doth open the back door to the Sphinx. It was all in the little book of sonnets. Where the key must fit in the wall to begin the journey to the stone. I was prepared to take the leap of faith. And I knew to find the stone and the stone's tablet here."

When Diesel and I found the first stone several months ago, we found a small tablet hidden with it. There was a power play between Diesel and Wulf, and Diesel got the stone but Wulf got the tablet. The tablet was written in an arcane language, but supposedly if the tablet could be translated it would lead to another stone.

"So why are you sitting here?" I asked Hatchet.

"When I returned to the secret entrance, it was closed and would not open. There was only silence. So I came back here to escape through one of the tunnels, but there is no escape I can find."

"I'm surprised Wulf would entrust you with the stone," I said. "I'd think he'd be the one to take possession of it."

"He could not identify it," Hatchet said. "Only you or I can identify the stone, and there are many stones here, as you can see. They could not all be brought back. It made sense that I would be the one to retrieve, and he would be the one to keep watch."

"We tried to get into the Sphinx, but

the back door was jammed," I told Hatchet. "The lock was smashed and the tip of what looked like your sword was wedged into it."

"I left my sword with my master," Hatchet said. "I fear harm has come to him at the hand of the she-devil Anarchy." He touched the gash on his head. "I met her here. She came from one of the many tunnels. She said she destroyed my liege lord and I was now her minion, but I refused. We fought, and she took the tablet and stone and ran into a tunnel, choosing unwisely."

"Which tunnel?" Diesel asked.

"The tunnel marked *N*. She was perhaps ten feet into the tunnel when it gave way and she dropped out of sight."

Diesel went to the tunnel and looked into the gaping hole. "It's a long way down."

"Do you see her?" I asked.

"No. I don't see a body."

"She's very strong," Hatchet said.

"Is this Deirdre Early we're talking about?" I asked him.

"I only know her as Anarchy."

"And she has the stone and the tablet?"

"Yes. I fear she does."

I looked at Diesel and his face showed nothing, but I knew he was thinking the same thing I was. Anarchy wouldn't know one stone from the next, and Hatchet would never give her the real stone. He'd keep the real stone on him and give her a substitute.

"There are four tunnels leading out," Diesel said. "We know we don't want to go in *N,* since it has a big hole in it. Did you try the other three?" he asked Hatchet.

"I did. And I always returned here."

"The tunnels are labeled *N, S, E, W,*" I said. "The points of the compass." I pulled a totally drenched piece of paper out of my jeans pocket and carefully unfolded it. "This is what I copied off The Key House plaque. It made no sense when I copied it, but now I'm thinking it might be the way out of this chamber."

Diesel took the paper from me. "It starts with *W.*"

Hatchet rushed to the *W* tunnel, and the rats ran with him.

"Dude," Diesel said to Hatchet. "You have to go last. I don't want to be stepping on your rats."

Hatchet retreated, and Diesel led the way into the tunnel. We turned a corner, the light disappeared, and we were plunged into darkness. I put my hand to Diesel's back and stayed close. I could hear Hatchet stumbling behind me, the rats squealing behind him.

Diesel stopped abruptly. I bumped into him, and Hatchet bumped into me, and I could feel the rats scurrying over my feet.

"Jeez Louise," I said, chills running down my spine, a scream lodged halfway in my throat.

Hatchet stepped back, and the rats went with him.

"A little advance notice next time you stop," I said to Diesel.

"Sorry. I forgot you can't see. There are two tunnel choices here. If we follow the letters on the plaque, we take *SW*, so here goes."

It's easy to lose track of time in the dark. Without a watch ticking off minutes, time either stretches on into infinity or flies, depending on your level of enjoyment. In this case, we seemed to be walking forever. Stopping while Diesel read the paper, and continuing on. We came to a small chamber where there was another crack in the high domed ceiling and weak light filtered down. I could see that there were two tunnel choices, and Diesel wasn't moving.

"Which way do we go?" I asked him.

"I don't know," Diesel said. "The ink is blurry on this one from the soaking. I wouldn't want to send us into a booby-trapped tunnel."

Some of the rats were abandoning Hatchet and wandering off into one of the tunnels.

"Follow the rats," I said. "Hopefully, they're heading for food."

In a couple beats, we were again without light. I was close behind Diesel, both hands clutching his shirt. Twice I felt something brush against my leg and I thought *rat!* And by this time, I was hoping it was a rat, because I didn't want to speculate what else it could be.

"I'm stopping," Diesel said. "We're at

a ladder. And I can see a hatch above it. Everyone stay here until I open the hatch."

I waited in the dark, listening to Diesel climb the ladder. There was a scraping sound, and Diesel told me to follow him. I climbed the ladder and Diesel lifted me out into a small dark chamber.

"I think we're behind a false wall," he said.

I felt him moving around, more scraping sounds, and the wall rotated to reveal a real room with a cement floor. Light was pouring through a couple half windows high on a cinder-block wall. Boxes and paint cans were stacked on one side of the room. Beyond the boxes, I saw what looked like a water heater.

"We're in a storeroom," Diesel said. "Either a classroom building or a dorm."

Diesel yelled to Hatchet to come up, and Hatchet climbed out and scrambled to his feet. One of the rats came with him. The rat looked around, and went back down the ladder. We closed the trapdoor and the rotating wall, and I punched Hatchet in the face.

"That's for Glo," I said.

Hatchet's nose was bleeding, and Diesel was smiling.

"Feel better?" Diesel asked me.

"No," I said.

I was no longer dripping, but my clothes were wet and smudged with mud from brushing against the dirt walls. Now that I wasn't quite so terrified, I was freezing.

"We need dry clothes," Diesel said. "Good thing credit cards are waterproof."

We left from a basement door. It was late afternoon and there was a definite chill in the air. We had emerged from the dorm behind the Sphinx.

"I will take my leave of thee now," Hatchet said. "I must search for my master."

"You can take your leave as soon as you give me the stone," Diesel said.

Hatchet feigned surprise. "Stone? What stone?"

"The Luxuria Stone," Diesel said. "You would never have given it to Anarchy. She had no way of knowing if it was enchanted."

"I never thought of that," Hatchet said. "I swear, I don't have the stone."

Diesel grabbed Hatchet, turned him upside down, shook him, and the stone dropped onto the ground. It was a plain little brown rock, very similar to the first stone Diesel and I found.

"Make sure it's enchanted," Diesel said to me.

"I'd rather not touch it," I said. "I'm not sure where he was storing it."

"Give me a break," Diesel said. "You've probably spent the last half hour walking on rat turds. Just pick the damn thing up."

"It was in my tunic," Hatchet said. "It wouldn't easily fit elsewhere."

I picked the stone up, and it hummed and vibrated in my hand and gave off heat. It wasn't just enchanted. It was *very* enchanted. I'd only felt stored energy this strong in one other instance, and that was when I'd held the other SALIGIA Stone.

"It's a SALIGIA Stone," I said to Diesel. "I can't tell if it's Luxuria."

Diesel set Hatchet on his feet. "Good

luck finding Wulf. We'll be in the Gap if you need us."

"That was nice of you to offer help," I said to Diesel.

"Not entirely. Anarchy has the tablet that always accompanies a stone. If she can translate the tablet, it'll give her the name of another SALIGIA guardian. And we'll be two steps behind in a race for that stone. I know nothing about Anarchy, except she might be Deirdre Early. Unfortunately, Early's house burned down, so I have no clue where to find her. Wulf, on the other hand, seems to be connected to her in some way."

We crossed Wheelock, walked past the Hopkins Center, The Hanover Inn, and turned onto Main Street. The Gap was on the left.

A couple heads turned when we walked in.

"Looks like you've been hiking the Appalachian Trail," one of the salesgirls said.

"Yeah, we slipped and fell in the river. We're shopping for dry clothes."

"Happens all the time," the girl said.

I gathered together everything I

needed, including a purse, and carted it all to the dressing room. I caught my reflection in the mirror on the way and my legs went rubbery. I looked worse than I'd imagined. New clothes would be a drop in the bucket. My face was filthy and my hair was freakshow.

Fifteen minutes later, Diesel and I walked out in nice dry clothes, our old clothes stuffed into plastic Gap bags.

Diesel was wearing jeans, a T-shirt, and a dark green cotton crew neck sweater with the sleeves pushed up.

"I like this look on you," I said. "Casual and rugged but civilized."

"I like your look, too," he said. "Pretty. And I can see the outline of your nipples."

We stopped in midstride on the sidewalk.

"Did I just say that out loud?" he asked.

"Yeah."

"I don't want to tell you what was left unsaid, but ripping your clothes off is part of it."

"It's the Lust Stone," I said. "Where's the stone?"

"It's in my jeans pocket."

"That's probably not a good location. Maybe you should put it in my new purse."

He took the stone out of his pocket and handed it over. "It might not be the stone. I've been thinking these thoughts ever since I met you."

I was glad he was attracted to me, but I was trying not to be overly flattered. I suspected Diesel wanted to rip the clothes off *lots* of women.

"What are we doing next?" I asked him.

"I thought we'd drop the bags off at the car, beyond that I don't know. I feel like there are too many loose ends. I don't like Anarchy wandering around above or below ground with the tablet."

"And Wulf?"

"I think it's odd he walked away from Hatchet when he knew Hatchet most likely had the stone."

"Maybe he's hurt. Maybe he got stung by a bee, or chased down the street by a bear, or crushed by a garbage truck."

Diesel smiled.

"Or maybe he had a run-in with Anarchy and came out the loser," I said.

"Wulf is a lot like me physically. It's not impossible, but it's very hard to do real damage to us. It's hard to imagine he'd come out the loser to Anarchy."

"She has the advantage of being crazy."

"I'm not convinced *Wulf* is entirely sane."

CHAPTER TWENTY-TWO

We dropped the bags in the car and walked back to the Sphinx. Hatchet was there, circling the building like a kid looking for his lost cat.

"No sign of Wulf?" Diesel asked him.

"I didst look everywhere. I fear the worst. His car hath not been moved."

"Maybe I can track him," Diesel said, walking away from the back of the building.

"I'm staying here," I told him. "Pick me up when you're done."

I sat on the steps to the Sphinx and watched the students. I'd never had the college experience. I'd gone to culinary school after high school, and I don't regret my choice. I love being a pastry chef. Still, I wondered what it would be like to be part of a college community.

The Sphinx steps weren't all that comfortable, and the students weren't terribly interesting. I stood and stretched and paced. I walked up the hill a little, looking for Diesel and Hatchet. No sign of either. I returned to the Sphinx, and when I passed by the back door I noticed that the tip of the sword was missing and the door was ever so slightly ajar.

I tentatively approached the door and opened it enough to see a crack of subdued light. I listened for movement inside. No sounds drifted out to me. I opened the door wider and peeked in.

"Hello?" I said. "Anybody home?"

I entered the building and recoiled at the sight of the body in the middle of what appeared to be a large kitchen. My initial reaction was confusion and horror. It was Wulf, and he was hog-tied. His body was bent backward at an extreme angle. His hands and feet were shackled and chained together. There was a rope wrapped around his neck and attached to the chains. He was blindfolded and there was duct tape across his mouth. And it looked to me like he was wired to a bomb that was also chained to a massive table.

I rushed to Wulf and ripped the blindfold and duct tape off him.

"Don't touch me," he said. "If I move, the bomb will go off."

"It has a digital clock attached," I told him. "It looks like it's set for a timed explosion."

"How much time do I have?"

"Almost five minutes."

"Leave. Get out of the building."

"What happens if I pull the wires off you?"

"If you do it in the right sequence you might defuse the bomb or at least free me from it. If you do it wrong the bomb will go off."

"What's the right sequence?"

"Only Anarchy knows that. And she's so insane, she might not even know the sequence. You need to leave *now*."

I looked at the digital display ticking away seconds, and I felt my scalp prickle. "The wires are color-coded. Does that mean anything to you?"

"No."

Damn! I looked at the open door, and I looked back at Wulf. I blinked back tears. "This really sucks," I said to him.

"It's okay," he said. "You need to leave and get as far from the building as possible."

"Can't do it," I told him.

There were two wires. Red and green. I ran to the counter, found a pair of shears, and ran back to Wulf.

I could feel sweat collecting in a pool between my breasts and rolling down the side of my face as I bent over Wulf and the wires. The time was ticking away. I had to make a decision. I pressed my lips together to keep from whimpering, said a small prayer, and slipped the strap to my shoulder bag over my head so the bag hung down my back and out of my way.

"Here goes," I said. "Go with green. I'm cutting the green one first."

I held my breath and snipped the wire. No explosion. My heart was racing and my nose was running. Some sweat dripped onto Wulf. "Sorry," I said. "I'm really scared." I had two minutes left, and I was working hard to keep my hands from shaking. I cut the red wire. Wulf was completely detached from the bomb, but the clock was running. I cut the rope attached to his neck, threw the shears away, grabbed the chains attached to Wulf, and dragged him to the door.

"Jeez Louise," I said, putting my weight behind it. "How much do you weigh?"

I managed to get to the door. I gave one last tug and we tumbled out. I yelled for help, and Diesel came running.

"Bomb!" I said. "Get him out of here."

Diesel and Hatchet picked Wulf up and we all ran about forty feet before the building exploded and we went flat to the ground. The back door and kitchen fan blew out and shot off like missiles. There was smoke and fire inside, but the exterior of the tomb looked intact and unscathed.

Diesel unlocked the shackles, and Wulf flopped onto his back and lay stretched out, spread-eagle, for a couple beats, breathing hard. Diesel gave Wulf a hand up, and we all moved away from the Sphinx. People were running from all directions and emergency vehicles were screaming down the street.

"What happened?" Diesel asked Wulf.

"Apparently, the ridiculous rumor that we should not have relations with our own kind is true. I met a woman who neglected to mention her special abilities to me. And now as time goes on she becomes more and more powerful, assuming my skills, and I'm left with very little. Obviously, I was the loser in this latest attempt to stop her."

"Anarchy," Diesel said.

"Yes. Also known as Deirdre Early. She's the heiress to the Early candy fortune. She has all the power and no ability to control it," Wulf said. "She was a monster in her own right, and I've created an even more powerful monster."

"Is there a way to uncreate her?" I asked him.

"Not easily," Wulf said.

"Sire," Hatchet said to Wulf, "perhaps if *we* had relations, I could obtain some of your skills and *I* could take over the business."

Wulf gave Hatchet a smack to the back of his head that knocked him to his knees. "I still have the strength to kill *you,*" Wulf said.

We were almost back to Marblehead, and I was struggling to keep my eyes open.

"Crawling around in dirt tunnels and swimming in grottoes is exhausting," I said to Diesel. "I'm going to bed early."

"And I'm sleeping on the couch," Diesel said. "That was a freaking sobering experience. It's not bad enough that Wulf is losing his power . . . the recipient went batshit."

"What are you going to do about her?"

"I'm going to try to locate her through the Early family. If no one's heard from her I'll go back into the tunnels to see if I can find her."

"She has the tablet."

"True," Diesel said, "but we have the stone."

"Omigosh!"

Diesel turned onto Washington Street. "I don't like the way that sounded. Should I be worried?"

"I don't have the stone."

"You lost the stone?"

"It was in my purse."

"And?"

"I don't have it. I think I left my purse in Hanover. I dropped it when the Sphinx exploded. And I sort of remember Hatchet picking it up, but then I turned my attention to Wulf."

Diesel gave a bark of laughter.

I rolled my eyes at him. "It's not funny!"

"I was thinking about Wulf going back to his car and discovering he had the Luxuria Stone. Here he is having a truly bad day. He's been chained to a bomb and left to die. Then he's rescued by a cupcake baker. And worst of all, he has to admit to us that he's lost his power. And just when he's thinking he's at the bottom, the Luxuria Stone drops into his lap."

"Life is strange," I said.

Diesel pulled into the parking area in front of my house, and we got out and stretched. Carl was sitting in the window, looking out at us, his face pressed to the glass.

"I must have been really terrible in a previous life to deserve Carl in this one," Diesel said.

"You like him."

"He's family," Diesel said. "He even looks like family. You should see my cousin Ralph."

Glo opened the door before we got to it. "How did it go? Were there more clues? Did you get the stone?"

"It's complicated," I said.

Diesel swung Carl up onto his shoulder. "We didn't get the stone, but we might know where it is."

"Where is it?"

"Wulf might have it," I said.

"Isn't that a bad thing?" Glo asked.

"It's not good," I told her. "How's it been here?"

"Quiet. I talked to Clara, and she's feeling okay. She's going to open the bakery tomorrow. I'm going in early to help with the bread, since she's supposed to be careful with her arm."

"How's *your* arm feeling?"

"It's fine. The cut wasn't super deep. It was more scary than anything else."

"What would you like to do about tonight? Would you like to stay here again?"

"No. I need to get home. And in case you're hungry, I had pizza delivered, and there's still a lot left. I got extra in case you wanted some."

Diesel took Glo home, and I went to the computer and researched Deirdre Early. I typed the name in and information poured onto the screen. Deirdre Early sitting in the front row during Fashion Week in New York. Deirdre Early dating a polo player, a rapper, a basketball player, a senator, her trainer, her pool boy. Deirdre Early arrested for protesting PETA in her sheared mink coat and nothing else.

She was the sole heir to the Early candy fortune. She'd been married three times and divorced three times. She had a 150-foot yacht that she kept in the Mediterranean. And her main residence was in Greenwich, Connecticut. I thought she seemed like the perfect date for Wulf, except that she was a homicidal maniac.

CHAPTER TWENTY-THREE

Diesel was asleep on the couch when I left the house at 4:30 A.M. He had one foot on the floor, one foot hanging over the armrest, and Carl was sleeping on his chest. It was endearing. I kissed him on his forehead, and he said, “See ya, Sunshine,” without ever opening his eyes.

No one accosted me on my way to Diesel’s car. I’d helped myself to his keys, and I hoped he didn’t want to go anywhere, because he wouldn’t have a car until I got off work.

Lights were on when I got to the bakery.

"How's the arm?" I asked Clara.

"I'm supposed to have it in a sling, but the sling drives me nuts. All the special orders for Monday have called in for today. I hope Glo gets here soon."

"She has an injury, too," I said. "Let me do the heavy lifting today. Glo can frost the cupcakes."

Twenty minutes later, Glo arrived.

"This isn't normal," Glo said. "Nobody gets up and goes to work at this hour. It's nighttime. Why don't we do the baking the afternoon before? Then we'd just have to put everything out in the racks and shelves when we open the store."

"It wouldn't be fresh," Clara said.

"Well, honest to goodness, how fresh does something have to be?" Glo said. "Mr. Nelson would never know the difference. Tell him his stupid pretzels are organic, so they might taste stale. You could charge him extra." She tied an apron on. "You'll never guess who called me last night after I got home. Hatchet. He wanted a date. He said he really enjoyed cutting me, but he wouldn't do it anymore if I didn't like it."

Clara and I were momentarily speechless.

"You aren't going out with him, are you?" Clara asked.

"I don't think so," Glo said. "He's a psycho-minion. Actually, that makes him a little interesting, but the whole poisonous snake thing puts me off."

"Get the pans ready," I said to Glo. "I'm starting the cupcakes."

At ten o'clock, Glo was helping a customer, Clara was pulling loaves of bread out of the oven, and I was whipping up a cauldron of buttercream frosting when Deirdre Early burst into the kitchen. Her face was smudged with dirt, her eyes were wild-woman, her hair was filthy and snarled, and her clothes were a mess.

"It's a fake," she said. "A fake!"

Glo rushed in from the store, and Clara and I snapped to attention.

"What's a fake?" I asked.

"The stone. That hideous Hatchet gave it to me. He said it was the Luxuria Stone, but I know it wasn't."

"How do you know?" I asked her.

"It doesn't do anything. I carried it around, and I felt nothing. And when I finally found my way out of the tunnel maze this morning, no one would talk to me. If it was the Luxuria Stone I was carrying, those college guys would be all over me, right? I mean, they'll hit on anything."

"You're sort of a fright," Glo said.

Early looked down at herself. "It wasn't easy getting out of that tunnel. There were bats and spiders, and I kept falling into holes."

"Do you have the tablet?" I asked her.

"I have half of it. It broke when I fell, and I could only find one piece in the dark. And it's not like I didn't look. I can't read the stupid thing anyway."

"If you want to give it to me, I might be able to find someone to read it," I told her.

"How about this. You give me the real stone, and I give you what I have of the tablet."

"Are you sure the stone isn't real?" I asked her.

"I hit it with a hammer." She pulled

some pulverized stone out of her pocket and dumped it on the floor. "If it was magic, it wouldn't break like this, right? What kind of magic stone breaks like this?"

We all shrugged.

"It's Hatchet," she said, her hands clenched, eyes narrowed.

Jars rattled on the pantry shelves and the building vibrated.

"I should have finished him off like I finished off Wulf. Mr. Look-at-me-because-I'm-so-sexy-and-powerful. He never even called the next day. We had this big hot date, and then nothing. What's with that? Even basketball players call me the next day. Or at least send flowers. Have some respect, you know? It's not like I didn't go to some effort. I was wearing La Perla."

"Bummer," Glo said. "That sucks. I hate when that happens. You know what's even worse? When they get shot with a nail gun and don't even show up."

Deirdre Early looked around. "I lost my focus. Why am I here?"

"Cupcakes," I said. "You want cupcakes."

"No. That's not it."

"A loaf of bread. This is a bakery," Clara said. "People come here for bread."

"No. It was something else."

"Hatchet?" Glo said.

"Yes! I *hate* Hatchet. He tricked me. I'd hate Wulf, too, but I killed him."

"Actually, he's still alive," I said.

She went still for a moment. "What?"

"He healed."

"That's impossible. I have all his power. I can cook an egg in the palm of my hand. I can hear grass grow. I can throw fire."

"I didn't know Wulf could throw fire," I said.

"It's this gadget I bought," Early said, pulling a propane torch out of her Hermès shoulder bag. "I bought it to caramelize crème brûlée, but you can torch anything with it."

"Your town house?" I asked.

"That was an accident."

"My car?"

"I was practicing. And how did I get all that flour on me? I can't remember."

"Flour?" Clara said. "What flour?"

I agreed. “I don’t remember any flour.”

Early pulled the trigger and—*whoosh*—about ten inches of blue flame shot out.

“Whoa,” Clara said. “That’s way beyond crème brûlée.”

“I like fire,” Early said, flicking the flamethrower, shooting out fire.

“So now what?” I asked her.

“World domination and chaos. My name is Anarchy!” she said, waving the torch around, shooting flames out at us. “What’s my name?” she asked us.

“Anarchy,” we said in unison.

“I want the stone, and *you* are going to get it for me.”

When she said *you*, she pointed at me and set my chef apron on fire. I batted at it with a kitchen towel, and Clara shot it with water from the sink hose.

“Jeez Louise,” I said, untying the wet apron, examining the hole in it. “Could you be more careful with that flamethrower! It’s not like aprons grow on trees.”

“You have twenty-four hours to get the stone to me, or I’ll burn your house to the ground,” she said.

She aimed the torch at a stack of towels and *phffffft*. Up in flames.

"I don't have the stone," I said to her. "Wulf has the stone."

Okay, that was a rotten thing to do to Wulf, but I didn't care. I was willing to throw him under the bus to get rid of Early or Anarchy or whoever the heck she was at the moment.

"Pay attention," she said. "I'm telling *you* to get it and bring it to me. You're making me angry."

Phfffft. She cremated a tray of soft pretzel rolls.

"You shouldn't have done that," Glo said. "Mr. Nelson's going to be in here any minute, and he's going to be pissed."

"I want that stone!" Anarchy shrieked.

"Sure," I said. "No problem. Where do you want it delivered?"

She pulled a card out of her purse. "This is my cell phone. I'm currently between addresses."

"Okeydokey," I said. "Would you like a cupcake for the road?"

"I don't eat cupcakes," she said. "Do I look like I eat cupcakes? I don't think so. I work glutes and abs seven days a week. I haven't got a single cellulite dimple. I eat like an alpaca. Sprouts and watercress."

"No wonder you're always so cranky," Glo said.

Phffft. Phfffft! She torched a roll of paper towels and three loaves of pumpernickel.

"She didn't mean *cranky,*" I said to Anarchy. "She meant sharp and focused. Eye of the tiger. Woman in charge." I looked over at Glo. "Right, Glo?"

"Yep," Glo said. "That's what I meant."

"Eye of the tiger," Anarchy said. "I like that." She looked around. "Why am I here?"

Clara bagged a loaf of multigrain and handed it to her. "You wanted bread."

"Oh yeah," Anarchy said. "Thanks."

And she left.

Clara closed and locked the door. "She's completely lost it. I'd like to get her some help, but I don't know where to begin."

"It's a problem," Glo said. "If you try to catch her with a big butterfly net like in a Three Stooges movie, she'll only set it on fire."

The bell jingled over the front door, and Glo took a quick peek into the shop. "It's Mr. Nelson," she said. "What should I tell him?"

"Tell him we're very sorry, but a batch got burned, so he's a little short this week. And give him as much as we have," Clara said. "Make up the difference with bagels."

"Do you think she'd really burn my house down?" I asked Clara.

"She burned her *own* house down. I think she'd burn *anything*."

I shoveled the cremated pretzels into a garbage bag and took the tray to the sink. "I can still smell burned bread and apron. It's like it's getting stronger. Now it smells like *rubber* burning."

BAROOOM!

Clara and I froze.

"Something exploded in the parking lot," I said. "I hope it was Anarchy."

Clara opened the door and looked out. "Did you drive Diesel's car to work?"

"Yes."

"You're going to need a ride home."

I could see the giant fireball from where I was standing.

"This isn't good," I said to Clara.

An hour later, the fire trucks pulled away and we now had two blackened, twisted hunks of dead vehicle in the parking lot.

"Lucky thing I parked on the street," Glo said, looking out the door at the wreckage. "What did Diesel say when you told him his car was toast?"

"He said he walked down the hill to the grocery store and got milk and cheese and cold cuts for lunch, but he'd like me to bring bread and a cheese Danish home."

"Nothing about the car?"

"He mumbled something about calling his assistant."

The front door jingled again, and Glo hurried off. She returned to the kitchen minutes later with a large vase of cut flowers.

"Someone sent me flowers!" she said. "I think it must be the bellringer." She opened the card that was attached and read the message. " 'Roses are red. Violets are blue. I doth think thou is hot. I hope thou doth thinkest I'm hot, too.' "

"Guess they aren't from the bellringer," Clara said.

"No," she said. "They're from Hatchet. He's nuts, but he's sweet." She put her face close to the flowers to smell the roses, and she shrieked and jumped back. "There's a big spider crawling around in the flowers."

"Probably meant as a pet," Clara said. She picked the vase up, carried it out to the parking lot, and set it next to the Dumpster. She came back inside and locked the door.

Diesel was hands in pockets, looking out my front window. "I think she's here with the car," he said.

"Your assistant?" I asked him.

"I don't know. I don't know what this latest one looks like."

"You still don't know her name, either, do you?"

Diesel grinned. "No. I keep meaning to ask."

She was pretty in a girl-next-door Miss America kind of way. Straight, shoulder-length, Jennifer Aniston blond hair, messenger bag hung on her shoulder, designer jeans, and a dressy little black jacket.

I went out to her and extended my hand. "I'm Lizzy Tucker. I work with Diesel."

"Mindy Smith," she said, shaking my hand. "I'm Diesel's assistant. He requested two cars. My associate should be coming right away. She was a couple minutes behind me." Mindy looked past me to the house. "Is Diesel here? I've never met him. I hear he's incredibly handsome."

"How long have you worked for him?"

"Three months. If I make it to six months, I'll get a hardship bonus. He has a reputation for being a little difficult."

I looked back at the house and crooked my finger at Diesel to come out.

"Was that him behind the curtain?" Mindy asked.

"Yes. He's very shy."

She hiked her bag higher on her shoulder. "Just goes to show how wrong rumors can be."

Diesel ambled out and Mindy sucked in some air. "Wow," she whispered.

"This is Mindy Smith," I said to Diesel. "Your assistant. Her associate is coming shortly with the second car."

"Nice," Diesel said.

Hard to tell if he was talking about the cars or about Mindy Smith.

"As you know, we try to get the best vehicles available," Mindy said, handing Diesel the keys to a black Aston Martin. "I hope this will be all right. The second car is identical to this one."

"I can make do," Diesel said.

"The papers are in the glove box. I've made arrangements to have your previous cars towed from the bakery parking lot. And I have the two new cell phones you requested."

The second car eased to a stop behind the first car, and a woman who looked like a Mindy Smith clone got out. She flushed a little at seeing Diesel, and for a moment I was afraid she was going to do something awful, like curtsy to the king. Fortunately, she pulled herself together and simply smiled and gave Diesel the second key.

"While you're here, you can help me out with one more thing," Diesel said.

He ran into the house, and minutes later he came out carrying the painting wrapped in a sheet, the Duane bell, and the Motion Machine.

"These need to be returned to their owners," he said. "There was a plaque that needed to go back as well, but it was stolen by a crazy lady."

Mindy took the painting, and her clone took the bell and the Motion Machine. Both women looked like deer in headlights, not sure what to do but unwilling to ask Diesel.

"Thanks," Diesel said to the women. "Have a good trip."

I followed Diesel into the house. "Where are they going? And how will they get there?" I asked him. "They haven't got a car."

"I guess they'll go back to the office, wherever that is."

"You don't know where the office is located?"

"No. Never had to go there."

I looked out the window. The women were gone.

"How? What?" I asked.

"They're very resourceful," Diesel said.

"Did they get beamed up or something?"

"You don't want to know. It would freak you out. Let's say someone gave them a ride."

Good enough for me.

"I've been instructed to defuse Anarchy," Diesel said. "She's made herself a sufficient nuisance to catch the attention of whoever makes these decisions."

"You don't know who makes the decisions?"

"I know some of the people involved. Their precise responsibilities aren't well defined. It's a blurry hierarchy."

"I have her cell phone number." I handed her card to Diesel. "She gave me twenty-four hours to get the stone to her, or else."

"Or else what?"

"She'll burn my house down."

"I'd hate that," Diesel said. "I like this house."

Diesel had the two cell phones that replaced the ones that had drowned. He gave one to me, and he punched

Anarchy's number into the other. She didn't answer.

"Probably getting her hair done and a manicure," I said.

"Do you have an address?"

"No. She said she was between addresses."

"No doubt."

"What all is involved in *defusing* someone?" I asked him.

"I can block certain kinds of destructive energy."

"Can you do that to Wulf?"

Diesel shook his head. "I've never been sanctioned to try. There are people in high places who protect Wulf." He looked at his watch. "I have an errand to run. Pack some sandwiches. When I get back, we're going on a field trip."

CHAPTER TWENTY-FOUR

I was buckled into the Aston Martin next to Diesel, and Carl was in the backseat. We'd been on the road for two hours, and I wasn't happy.

"This is a dumb idea," I said to Diesel.

"It's a loose end that has to be tied."

"Yeah, but why do I have to tie it? Why can't you tie it all by yourself?"

"Where would the fun be in that? Besides, I can't do this without you. I'm not going to all this aggravation only to bring home something worthless."

We were going back to Dartmouth to try to retrieve the half tablet Anarchy dropped in the tunnel. I couldn't argue over the value of the tablet. If it could be deciphered, it would give us a head start on finding the next stone. At least it would give us half a head start. Anarchy still had the other half.

The legend is that a tablet accompanied each stone and gave the name of another guardian family. It was the way families were able to find one another over the centuries if disaster struck.

My problem was that I flat-out did not want to go back underground. And I thought this whole search-and-rescue mission smacked of wild-goose chase. What were the chances of finding half of a tablet in the endless, dark, confusing tunnels?

"I wish you would stop sighing and harrumphing," Diesel said. "It's starting to creep me out."

"Well, excuse me, but this moronic mission is creeping *me* out. And I'm not diving into that pool of black water. I'll wait at the end of the tunnel. You can bring the tablet to me if you can find it."

"We're not going in that way. We're going in the way we came out."

"It was a maze. We'll get lost and die. And there were rats! Remember the rats?"

"We won't get lost. The tunnels were marked. We'll be fine if we read the markings going in and going out. And I've taken precautions."

"What kind of precautions?"

"Spray paint and rope."

"Oh boy."

We pulled into Hanover a half hour later. The sun had just set, but there was still lots of light. Students were on the move to and from dorms, going to eat, heading for the library.

Carl was making restless sounds in the back, anxious to get out of the car.

"What are you going to do with Carl while we're in the tunnels?" I asked Diesel.

"He's coming with us. I have a leash."

"Eeep?" Carl said.

I contemplated my life choices and wished I had something calming and comforting. Catholics have rosaries and things they can chant, but I was raised Presbyterian, and we have bupkis. I guess there's prayer, but that takes some thought. Smoking would be another way to go. Smokers always look so happy when they suck on a cigarette. I might even be willing to risk lung cancer, but the wrinkly, oxygen-deprived skin issue is a big turnoff. And I'd hate to smell like my Aunt Rose, who died with a Marlboro Light hanging from the corner of her mouth. Although they tell me she died smiling.

We found a parking place on the side street by the tennis courts and walked across Wheelock to the Sphinx. Diesel had his backpack filled with the rope and spray paint, and I had Carl. He was wearing his new harness, designed for a dog but it fit Carl just fine, and his leash was attached. We skirted the fire-smudged Sphinx on our way up the hill. The back door had been replaced and the small exhaust fan that was high on the back wall had also been replaced.

There were students talking by the bike racks in front of our target dorm. We kept our distance and walked around the end of the three-building cluster. We stopped a short distance from the basement door and watched the activity. No one was on this side of the building. Good thing for that, because it's hard to blend in when you've got a monkey.

"Showtime," Diesel said.

We casually crossed to the door, Diesel opened it, and we slipped inside and quickly walked through the revolving wall to the trapdoor. I went down the ladder first, Carl followed, and Diesel came last, closing the hatch, plunging us into darkness.

I felt something scurry across my foot, and in a flash Carl was off the ground and sitting on my head.

I could hear Diesel pulling things out of the backpack. He switched on a light and handed it to me.

"Put this on," he said.

"What is it?"

"It's a headlamp. Hikers use them. It'll give you hands-free light."

I put the headlamp on and watched while Diesel fixed one onto Carl.

"Where did you find one to fit Carl?" I asked him.

"Ace Hardware. They have everything."

Diesel put his headlamp on and attached a Maglite to the waistband of his jeans. He coiled a long length of rope over his shoulder and grabbed a can of fluorescent yellow spray paint.

"Let's go," he said. "Stay close."

Stay close was advice I didn't need. As it was, I couldn't get close enough. The only one more unhappy than me to be in the dark, dank tunnel was Carl. He was clinging to me with his monkey fingers curled into my shirt in a death grip.

In some ways, it had been better to blindly follow Diesel in the dark last time. I hadn't seen the spiders hanging from webs above our heads or the dirt sifting down from rotting support beams. When we came to a fork in the tunnel system, Diesel looked for the letter chipped into the stone marker, and he spray painted the walls at the entrance to the tunnel we were about to exit, to make sure we'd make no mistake on the way out.

We came to the small chamber with the domed ceiling. No sunlight filtering through this time. The sun had set. Diesel moved through the room and took us into more tunnels.

If I looked around Diesel, I could see

something reflecting light at the end of the current tunnel. Quartz crystals, I thought. We'd finally reached the large domed room where we'd found Hatchet. The room where the stone and the tablet had resided.

I stepped into the room and felt a sense of relief. It was still claustrophobic, but at least I wasn't moving through narrow dirt tunnels.

Carl looked around and slowly climbed down. He stood for a moment, testing the dirt-and-stone floor.

"Eeh," he said.

We'd emerged from the tunnel marked *W,* now spray painted yellow. There were five tunnel entrances opening into the room. We knew from Hatchet that the *N* tunnel had been booby-trapped.

Diesel went to the *N* tunnel and peered into the dark hole with his Maglite.

"What do you see?" I asked him.

"Nothing. No tablet on the ground that I can see. I'd say it's around a twenty-foot drop."

The floor of the domed room was littered with small brown rocks the same size and shape as the Luxuria Stone.

Mixed with the small brown rocks were chunks of crystal like the ones embedded in the walls and ceiling. I picked up a couple of the prettier crystal chunks and put them in my sweatshirt pocket.

"She said she fell multiple times," I told Diesel.

"Let's hope she lost the tablet on the first fall."

I went to the hole and looked in. "You might be able to drop down and only break one or two bones, but you have no way of getting out, other than wandering around for a couple days."

"I'm not going down. That's the genius of my plan. Carl's going down."

Carl's eyes went wide open. "Eeeep!"

"I brought rope," Diesel said, slipping the coil of rope off his shoulder. "I figure we tie the rope to Carl's harness, and we lower him down. When he finds the tablet, we bring him back up."

Carl was shaking his head no so hard I was afraid his eyes would pop out and roll around on the ground.

"It's perfectly safe," Diesel said to Carl. "I'll have a good grip on you. It could even be fun. You'll get to see a new tunnel."

Carl gave Diesel the finger.

Diesel tied the rope to the back of Carl's harness, picked Carl up by it, and bobbed Carl up and down like a yo-yo.

"Good to go," Diesel said.

"He looks worried."

Diesel hung him over the hole. "Nothing to worry about. What could go wrong?"

"Eeeeee," Carl said, descending into the abyss, holding tight to his harness, feet dangling, his mini-headlamp shining into the darkness.

"Remember, you're looking for the tablet," Diesel called to Carl. "I'll pull you up when you get the tablet."

I stood back a couple feet and manned the Maglite. I was trying to illuminate the ground below, but it was difficult to get the beam of light past Carl.

"He's on the ground," Diesel said. "The rope went slack. I think he's walking around. "Hey, Carl!" he called down. "How's it going? Do you see the tablet?"

"Chee," Carl said, his voice very faint.

Moments later, there was a tug on the rope. Carl wanted to come up.

"Did you get the tablet?" Diesel asked.

"Chee."

Carl had something in his hands coming up. Impossible to see what it was—my light was throwing shadows. Diesel lifted Carl out of the hole and swung him toward me. Carl had a dead rat.

"Eeep?" Carl asked, holding the rat out for me to see.

"Dude, that's not a tablet," Diesel said.

Carl dropped the rat, and Diesel kicked it over the edge into the hole.

"Back you go," Diesel said, sending Carl down, down, down.

"Eep," Carl said.

The rope went slack and then played out.

"He's walking around," Diesel said.

Diesel leaned over the edge to see better, and the dirt gave way.

"Oh crap," Diesel said, tumbling into the hole.

WHUUUMP! Diesel landed on his back far below me.

"Omigod," I said. "Are you okay?"

"I think I landed on the rat."

"As long as you didn't land on Carl."

Carl jumped onto Diesel's chest and gave me a big monkey smile and a finger wave.

Diesel got to his feet and looked around.

"Do you see the tablet?" I asked him.

"Yes," he said. "It's partially covered by dirt. It's no wonder Carl couldn't find it."

"So what are you going to do now?" I asked him. "How are you going to get back here?"

"I'm not. There's no way."

"But I'm here," I said.

"You'll have to go back by yourself, and I'll find my way out."

"What? Are you crazy? I'm not walking back through all those tunnels by myself!"

"It's easy," Diesel said. "They're spray painted. The only other option is to come down here."

I looked over the edge. "It's a long way."

"I'll catch you."

"Anarchy said there were spiders and bats that way."

"And?"

"I don't like spiders and bats."

"You have to choose."

"Okay, I'm coming down."

"Great."

I was on the edge of the hole, but I couldn't bring myself to jump. I'd start, but then I'd chicken out.

"Oh, for the love of Pete," Diesel said.

I glared down at him. "This is all your fault. This was your stupid idea. And then you went and fell in the hole. What the heck were you thinking?"

"I was thinking I had to get the tablet."

"Even your monkey knew it was a bad idea, but did you listen to him? No, no, no."

"Women," Diesel said to Carl. "Can't live with them. Can't live without them."

"Ugh!" I said. "Idiot! I'll meet you at the car."

I turned and huffed off to the *W* tunnel, put my head down, and stomped and swore, following the yellow splotches. "Stupid, stupid, stupid!" I said. "I can't believe I got talked into this harebrained idea." A spider as big as a silver dollar dropped onto my arm, and I backhanded it off into the black beyond. "Special abilities, my foot. Enhanced senses. See where that gets you. For sure not out of a twenty-foot hole. At least I can make cupcakes." I passed through the smaller domed room, and several sets of glittery little eyes reflected light from my headlamp. The eyes started to move toward me and I yelled at them. "Do *not* mess with me. I'm not in a good mood. *Shoo!*"

I marched through yet another tunnel, on a rant about Diesel and rats and roaches, and I looked ahead and saw the ladder. I was up the ladder and out the trapdoor and revolving door in a heartbeat. I took my headlamp off, ran my hands through my hair, and shook myself to make sure I didn't have hitchhikers. I took a minute to calm myself, and then I left the building and walked out into the night air.

By the time I got to the car, I was worrying about Diesel and Carl. Diesel was down there without a map or yellow paint splotches to guide him. He was a big, strong guy. He was brave. He was smart. He could block bad energy and do who knows what else. None of that would help if a tunnel caved in.

An hour later, I was still waiting. I watched my cell phone for a text message, and I tried calling Diesel's phone. Nothing turned up on either. I was cold and I was scared. The car was locked. My purse was inside the car. A man and a monkey I loved, at least some of the time, were trapped underground. I decided I'd give Diesel until ten o'clock, and then I'd get people into the tunnels to search for him.

A little after nine, I was sitting on the curb by the Aston Martin, and I felt hands at my waist and was lifted to my feet.

"I was worried about you," Diesel said, wrapping his arms around me, holding me close. "I should have been more careful."

He kissed me, and just when it was getting really interesting, Carl climbed up my back and sat on my head.

Diesel took Carl off my head and remoted the car open. "I was afraid you might leave without me."

"I didn't have a car key."

Diesel opened the door for me. "Is that the only reason?"

"Of course not. I wouldn't leave Carl stranded."

Carl rushed into the car and jumped into the backseat. Carl was ready to go home.

I blew out a sigh. "I wouldn't leave you stranded, either."

"You were worried about me," Diesel said.

"Yes."

Diesel handed the broken tablet to me. It was marble, with engraved writing, and if it had been whole, it would have been the size of a legal envelope.

"Is this the tablet?" he asked me.

"I can't say for certain, but chances are very good. Its energy is identical to that of the stone."

CHAPTER TWENTY-FIVE

"You've been frozen in one spot, staring into that bowl of frosting, for the last ten minutes," Clara said to me. "Are you asleep?"

"I had a late night. I don't know how I used to do it when I worked restaurant shifts and got by on four hours of sleep."

The back door opened and Glo walked in. She dropped her messenger bag on the floor, along with Broom and her jean jacket, and she shuffled off to get her bakery smock.

"I'm done," Glo said. "I didn't sleep all night. I need coffee."

Clara wiped her hands on a towel. "I could swear I hear music."

"It's Hatchet," Glo said. "He followed me here. I can't get rid of him. He was outside my window all night, playing his lute and singing embarrassing songs to me. I couldn't get him to stop. If he keeps this up, I'm going to get evicted."

Clara and I went to the door and looked out at Hatchet. He was dressed up in his Sunday best, wearing a slouchy green velvet hat with a big plum-colored plume.

"O Glo, O Glo, I love thee so," he sang. He strummed a couple notes on his lute and bowed to us. "I bid thee morning, fair women. Wouldst fair Glo wish to hear my tune?"

"No!" Glo yelled from inside the kitchen. "Go away!"

"She jests," Hatchet said. "Glo is witty. Glo is pretty. Glo doth make my heart sore, my manhood sing."

Clara closed and locked the back door.

"I'm going to throw up if I have to hear any more about his manhood," Glo said.

"It's just wrong to be singing about it while you're playing a lute."

She went to the front shop, turned the CLOSED SIGN TO OPEN, and unlocked the front door. I brought out the last tray of cupcakes and transferred them into the display case, and spotted Hatchet on the sidewalk. I could see him through the front window, strumming and singing to people passing by.

"My love's lips of cherry make me merry. Turgid nipples and tongue like a cat. I'd doth give her my hat for one hot kiss. Kiss, kiss, I miss my Glo," Hatchet sang.

Glo looked down at herself. "What's a turgid nipple? Is it good?"

Mrs. Kramer bustled into the bakery. "There's a strange man outside singing about turgid nipples." She looked at Glo. "I think he's singing about *your* turgid nipples."

Glo stormed out of the bakery and yelled at Hatchet. "Stop it this instant. You have no business singing about my nipples. You've never even seen them. And besides, nipples are private. How would you like it if I sang songs about your johnson?"

"I would like it," Hatchet said.

"If you keep this up, I'm going to turn Broom loose on you."

"How doth my johnson love thee?" Hatchet sang. "Let me count the ways. Upside down and round and round . . ."

Glo stomped back into the bakery and slammed the door shut.

"I'd like a loaf of seeded rye, sliced," Mrs. Kramer said. "And two strawberry cupcakes."

Diesel rolled into the bakery at noon, looking fresh as a daisy.

"You slept all morning, didn't you?" I asked him.

"Not *all* morning." He helped himself to coffee. "I see you have a minstrel today. I had my window down when I drove by, and he was singing about Glo's fuzzy peach cheeks."

Glo opened the bakery door and threw a bagel at Hatchet. It hit him in the head and knocked his hat off.

"Stop it!" Glo shouted at him. "I *hate* you."

Mr. Ryan followed Glo back inside. "Do you have any cheese Danish left?"

"Sure," Glo said. "How many would you like?"

"I hate to take you away from all this fun," Diesel said, "but I have a meeting set up with Anarchy, and I need you to come with me."

"Now?"

"I'm meeting her in the parking lot of the Waterfront Hotel. It shouldn't take long. I'll bring you back here after."

I looked over at Clara. "Is that okay?"

"Yes. You're done baking, and you can do cleanup when you get back. Take whatever time you need."

"I'd really appreciate it if you'd jump the curb and run over Hatchet for me," Glo said.

Diesel smiled at her. "He's in love."

I changed out of my chef coat, grabbed my shoulder bag, and we went out to the car.

"Why do I have to go with you? Do you need a witness to the defusing?"

"I'm not doing any defusing. The request has been withdrawn."

"Why?"

"I suspect it has to do with Wulf. Technically, Anarchy has his power, and maybe he thinks he can get it back somehow."

"Can't you take it away from her and give it back to Wulf?"

"That's not in my skill set."

"Then why are we meeting with her?"

"I spoke to her this morning and told her we were ready to trade her half of the tablet for the real stone."

"You don't have the real stone."

"She doesn't know that," Diesel said.

"When she finds out she's been tricked again, she's going to burn my house down."

"Honey, she was going to burn your house down anyway."

I felt my face screw up into a grimace.

"Don't look so worried," Diesel said. "I won't let her burn your house down. Where would I sleep? Where would I eat?"

"Your own apartment?"

Diesel turned off Derby Street into the

hotel parking lot. This was the middle of October, and it was crazy time in Salem. The streets were packed with gawkers, zombies, witches, and ghouls arriving early for Halloween. They came by chartered bus, hired limo, junker, and SUV. They mingled with the locals, some of whom already were a little nutty on their own, in the bars and shops, and they marched in the streets.

About twenty zombies were gathered in front of the hotel, most likely waiting for a tour bus. Anarchy was standing apart, closer to the waterfront, and she looked more like one of the zombies than like Dierdre Early. She was dressed in something Catwoman might wear, except without the mask with the ears. Her short black hair was slicked back. Her lips were bloodred. Her eyes were black-rimmed with heavy liner, and some of it had smeared. Hard to tell if the smears were by accident or design.

"Do you have a rock for her?" I asked him.

"It's here on the console."

I looked at the rock. It was very similar to the real thing. Smooth, small, brown.

"This is the wrong rock," I said to him. "Her last rock looked like this, and she smashed it with a hammer." I searched in my bag for the crystal I'd picked up in the grotto. "She can't tell if the rock is empowered, and she doesn't really know what it's supposed to look like." I found the crystal and held it out to him. "I put this in my purse just in case we needed it. Give her something pretty that looks like it would have some value."

"Smart," Diesel said. "I like it."

We parked and walked over to Anarchy, and the closer we got, the creepier she looked. There was a quality to her face that whispered hysteria. Her pupils were shrunken to pinpoints. Her mouth was hard and compressed. Her manicure was perfect.

"I told you she got a manicure," I whispered to Diesel.

We stopped a few feet from her. "Do you have the tablet?" Diesel asked.

She reached into her black leather bag and took the cracked half of the tablet out.

"Well?" Diesel asked me.

I put my fingertip to the engraved piece of marble. "Affirmative."

"Do you have the stone?" Anarchy asked.

Diesel held the crystal in the palm of his hand for her to see.

"How do I know this is real?" Anarchy asked.

"Doesn't it look real?" I asked her. "It's beautiful. It has the power of the crystal. Touch it. You'll be able to feel the heat."

She touched the stone. "I can feel it! It's warm."

It was warm because it had been in Diesel's hot hand, but no need to go into details. Anarchy gave Diesel the tablet, and he gave her the stone.

"So you're not going to burn my house down, right?" I asked her.

"I couldn't be bothered," Anarchy said. "Your house is inconsequential."

"Absolutely," I said. "It's not worth your time. Just checking."

We returned to the Aston Martin and watched the zombies step single file into a trolley.

"They're good zombies," Diesel said. "Orderly."

Hatchet was gone when Diesel dropped me off at the bakery. Clara was taking refrigerator and storage cabinet inventory. Glo was tidying up the glass cases in the front shop. And I had my station to clean. I tied an apron around myself and got to work, enjoying the tedium and satisfaction of the job. Saving the world gets old pretty quick. I'd rather scrub a cake pan any day of the week. Although it was sort of fun to see Anarchy get excited about the crystal. I'd almost wished it was real.

The front door jingled, and a moment later, Glo appeared, wide-eyed and breathless.

"He's here! In the shop!"

"Who?" Clara asked.

"Wulf," Glo said. "He wants to talk to Lizzy."

I dried my hands and went out front, keeping the counter between Wulf and me. I assumed he was still in a weakened condition, but I didn't know exactly what that meant, because he didn't look weak. He was in his usual perfectly tailored black, and he looked as powerful as ever.

"Walk with me," he said.

I followed him outside and around the corner, where the foot traffic was nonexistent.

"I'm in your debt," Wulf said. "I'm giving the stone back to you as partial payment."

I took the stone and my purse from him and felt the power radiate up my arm. "I'm happy to get the stone back, but you don't owe me anything."

"I owe you my life. Unfortunately, your selfless act seems to have changed the stone. Whether it's changed it completely and permanently remains to be seen. For now, it appears to have lost much of its intriguing evil properties of lustful wanting and gained the undesirable ability to make some people believe in true love."

"That's a good thing."

"It's boring and useless. And its influence has turned my minion into a worthless, slobbering romantic. He's convinced he's in love with your counter girl."

"And you?" I asked. "Have you been affected by the stone?"

"It would be difficult to tell," Wulf said. "I've always been a romantic. I've seen *Casablanca* twice, and I sat through the entire ordeal of *Titanic*."

"Didn't you enjoy *Titanic*?"

"I was relieved when the ship went down."

Wulf had a sense of humor, sort of. Who would have thought.

"Are you going to disappear in a flash of light and a cloud of smoke?" I asked him.

"I hadn't planned on it," Wulf said. "My car is here. I was going to *drive* away. Are you disappointed?"

"A little."

He swept his arm out, there was a flash of light and a lot of smoke, and when the smoke cleared Wulf was gone. So was his car.

That's one heck of a parlor trick, I thought.

Glo and Clara were waiting for me when I went back into the bakery.

"What was that about?" Clara asked.

I told them about the stone and how it had changed and was no longer of any use to Wulf.

"So instead of the Lust Stone, it's the True Love Stone," Glo said. "That's so cool. We should take it out tonight for a test-drive. I might be able to find *the one*."

"I thought the bellringer was the one," Clara said.

"Me, too. He had real potential, but it turned out he was married. And he wasn't even a bellringer. He was a janitor."

"How does the stone work?" Clara wanted to know. "Is it like a Ouija board, telling you yes, or no, or forget about it? Does it sniff out your soul mate? Does it make you fall in love?"

"I don't know," I said. "It didn't come with instructions."

"We should definitely take it out," Glo said.

"I agree," Clara said. "It's been sitting around for centuries, probably. It needs a night out."

CHAPTER TWENTY-SIX

Diesel texted me saying he'd be home for dinner but not much before. I thought this was a nice change from having him pick me up at work and drag me off on a hunt for some enchanted relic. When I got to Marblehead, I stopped to get groceries and a bottle of wine. I let myself into my house, said hello to Cat and Carl, and took a moment to enjoy the quiet. I set the SALIGIA Stone on the kitchen counter and put the food away. By the time Diesel walked in, I had the table set and a steak ready to go on the grill.

"Where were you?" I asked him.

"I took the tablet to the office."

"You found out where the office is located?"

"Yeah. Turns out it's in Quincy. At least that's where it was today." He paused and looked at the SALIGIA Stone. "Is that what I think it is?"

"Wulf gave it back to me. He said I changed the stone when I helped him, and now it's an icky True Love Stone."

"He said 'icky True Love Stone'?"

"Not in those words, but I knew what he meant. And he said he owed me, and this was partial payment for his debt."

"I wish I'd known. I could have taken the stone with me to Quincy."

"You can't take it yet. I promised Glo and Clara we could take the stone out tonight to see if we could find true love."

"Let me get this straight. You have a priceless, powerful relic that has been carefully guarded for centuries, and you're going to take it to a bar to see if it gets you hooked up?"

"More or less."

"That's impressive."

After dinner, I changed into my best

jeans and a black V-necked sweater. I put on some slut makeup, slipped my feet into high-heeled ankle boots, and hung big hoop earrings from my ears.

"The stone is going to be overkill for you tonight," Diesel said. "You're not going to have any trouble finding true love in those jeans and that sweater. In fact, you might find it if you stayed home."

A horn beeped outside.

"That's Clara," I said. "She's picking me up. She's the designated driver."

Diesel went to the door with me. "Be good."

I grabbed my jacket and my shoulder bag and ran to the car.

"Do you have it?" Glo asked when I got in.

"It's in my purse."

"Can I see it?"

I hauled the stone out.

"It's sort of ugly," Glo said. "It's just a plain old rock. Are you sure it's special?"

"Yes. And we have to guard it with our lives. And we can't tell anyone we have it."

Clara drove out of Marblehead and

took Derby Street to Bum's Sports Bar. There were lots of televisions playing various sporting events that no one was watching. High-top tables and stools. And a long bar that was packed with zombies and werewolves. We elbowed our way into the bar, and Glo and I got a beer, and Clara got a Coke.

"Okay, so here's the deal," I said. "I'm not sure what the stone is supposed to do, so I guess we stand here and see if it radiates anything from inside my purse."

"I think I'm feeling something," Glo said. "I might be in love with the werewolf next to me."

Clara and I looked over at him.

"He seems like your average werewolf," Clara said.

The werewolf picked up on our attention and turned to us. "Arwoooh," he said. "Are you looking for someone?"

"Sort of," Glo said.

"Well, how do you feel about dogs? I can go from furry to naked in 1.3 seconds."

"Now I remember why I never do this," Clara said.

"How about you?" Glo asked, turning from the werewolf to me. "You're the one carrying the stone. Do you have romantic feelings for any of these zombies?"

"Not yet."

I didn't have feelings for the zombies, but I was feeling cuddly for someone I couldn't completely identify. Diesel, maybe. Or possibly Brad Pitt.

We stuck it out for another twenty minutes. There was a lot of hooking up going on, but not for us.

"I think the stone is a dud," Glo said. "I have better luck on my own."

"Maybe it's that the stone finds true love, and our true love isn't here," I said. "If it was still the Luxuria Stone inspiring lust, we'd be in the right spot."

"This is sort of embarrassing, but I had some lust for Wulf today," Glo said.

"I had lust for Andy Sklar," Clara said.

Glo chugged her second beer. "Isn't he the guy who comes in every day and gets a banana muffin?"

"Yeah," Clara said. "I think he's cute."

They looked at me.

"Diesel," I said. "I have a lot of lust for Diesel."

They both knew I couldn't do the deed with Diesel.

"Forbidden fruit," Clara said.

We left the bar and stepped outside, where the Halloween crazies were parading up and down the sidewalk.

"There are more trolls than usual this year," Clara said.

I was relatively new to Salem, and I had a hard time telling trolls from ghouls. For that matter, I had a hard time with the whole Halloween obsession. I mean, I like Halloween, but this was Halloween gone gonzo.

"The Exotica Shoppe is open late tonight," Glo said. "It's only a block away. Could we check on my frickberry?"

We walked the block to the Exotica Shoppe, and I held tight to my handbag the whole way. I was feeling the responsibility of the stone, thinking I'd done a dumb thing. What if I was attacked by a purse snatcher? What if Anarchy somehow discovered the crystal wasn't the SALIGIA Stone, and she was out looking for me? What if my absorption of the stone's power hits critical mass and I find my true love? And now for the really scary part—what if it's Wulf?

We entered the store and found Nina asleep with her head on the counter next to the register.

"Hello," Glo said. "Anybody home?"

Nina picked her head up and blinked at us. "I must have dozed off. It's been slow tonight. Lots of people outside, but no one coming in."

"Well, *we're* here," Glo said. "Did the frickberry come in?"

"Yes. I have it here with your name on it." Nina reached under the counter and pulled out a small bag. "Remember not to overdo this. A pinch is all you need."

"Do you have any arcane cookbooks?" Clara asked.

Nina adjusted her bejeweled princess crown. "I have a couple in the book section in the far corner, behind the Harry Potter wand and feather boa display."

We all migrated to the book section.

"I could spend the whole night here looking through books," Glo said. *"The Little Book of Pleasant Potions, An Anthology of Sixteenth-Century Witches,*

How to Brew Your Own Beer, 101 Ways to Use Batwing."

Clara was paging through a small leather-bound book. "This is a replica of a book printed in 1534. It's an entire book of marzipans and sweets."

It was difficult to see the front of the store from where we were standing, too many free-standing shelves in the way. I heard the front door open and close and the tap of high-heels on Nina's wood floor. Curiosity got the better of me, and I peeked around a shelf to see the vampire, zombie, witch, or whatever who had just entered.

It was Anarchy. She was still dressed in the black leather body suit. Her makeup was still fright-night. From where I was standing, I could see that Nina's back had gone rigid. Obviously, she recognized Anarchy from the last time she was in.

"I need something to enhance power," Anarchy said to Nina. "I recently acquired some new skills, but they seem to be leaking away."

"Were these skills the result of a spell or potion?" Nina asked.

"No. They were the result of physical contact. Does it matter?"

"It might." Nina pulled a small bottle off the rack behind her. "This is a performance enhancer. Very effective, I'm told. It contains a small amount of steroid." She selected a second bottle. "This is organic powdered hoof of unicorn, and it's frequently used to enhance abilities. It can also be used to make aspic."

"There's no such thing as a unicorn."

"That's what it says on the label." Nina showed her the bottle. "It's a very reliable company."

"Fine. Wrap them up," Anarchy said. "I'll figure it out later." She looked around. "I'm planning on world domination and mass chaos. I might need large quantities of hallucinogenic substances. Can that sort of thing be ordered by bulk?"

"Of course," Nina said. "We special-order all the time." Nina looked in my direction and did a whirly index finger next to her head.

Anarchy examined the jar of unicorn hoof. "How long does it take this to work?"

"It works pretty fast," Nina said. "Mix it with a little orange juice. And you might want to add frickberry to prolong the effect."

"Great. Give me some frickberry."

Glo and Clara were spying on Anarchy, too, at this point.

"It's a shame I didn't have frickberry when I froze her," Glo whispered.

Anarchy unscrewed the jar of unicorn hoof. She stuck her finger in and tasted some of the powder. "If this doesn't work, I'm going to come back and burn your store down," she told Nina. "I'm actually on my way to burn someone's house down now."

"Anyone I know?" Nina asked.

"Some insignificant cupcake baker who lied to me. Thought I could be tricked into believing I was getting something when I was getting nothing."

"How do you know you got nothing?" Nina asked.

"I've had no reaction to this fraudulent object."

"Isn't burning someone's house down extreme?"

"It's only the beginning. When I find

her, I'm going to extract her liver and feed it to feral cats."

I pulled Glo and Clara back behind the shelf. "Sneak out and get help. And call Diesel. I'm not getting any bars on my cell phone in here. Go to the street and call him, and tell him to come to the Exotica Shoppe to collect Anarchy. I don't care if he's authorized or not. I'll stay here and keep my eye on her."

"I don't want to leave you here," Clara said. "She wants to feed your liver to feral cats."

"I'll be okay. I'll stay hidden. Go!"

"Will there be anything else?" Nina asked Anarchy.

"I hear whispering," Anarchy said, looking around. "Who else is here?"

"It's this old building," Nina said. "It whispers."

There was the sound of the front door opening and closing, and I knew it was Clara and Glo leaving the shop.

"And the wind rattles the door sometimes, too," Nina said.

Even from this distance, I could see the insanity sweep over Anarchy.

"Liar," she said, her voice cold, her

eyes crazy. “There’s someone else here.” She pulled her torch out of her Gucci hobo bag and waved it at Nina. “Tell me, and I might not set you on fire. Although, it would be fun to see that Glinda the Good Witch gown go up in flames.”

“I don’t know,” Nina said. “I fell asleep. Someone might have come in.”

Anarchy shot out ten inches of blue flame, and the puffy net veil attached to Nina’s princess crown caught fire. Nina pulled the crown off and stomped on it.

“Help!” Nina yelled.

“Shut up,” Anarchy said. “No one’s going to help you in time.”

Nina reached her hand into a jar on the counter and threw some gray powder at Anarchy. “Go away. Go away.”

“What the heck?” Anarchy said.

“It’s deathweed,” Nina said. “It’ll make you shrivel up and blow away.”

Anarchy looked down at herself. She wasn’t shriveling.

“Maybe I grabbed the wrong jar,” Nina said. “Was it gray powder or red powder?”

“Gray powder,” Anarchy said.

"Oops, my bad. That was powdered dragon horn. It's a diuretic."

Anarchy moved through the shop with her torch in her hand. "I know someone's here. I can hear breathing. I can feel a heartbeat."

I was crouched down behind the bookcase, trying to control my breathing. The heartbeat I couldn't do much about. My heart was pounding in my chest. I heard her turn in my direction, heard the heels coming closer, and then there she was, looking down at me.

"You!" she said. "How convenient."

She waved the torch at me, and I jumped away.

"You need to calm yourself," I said. "You should have Nina mix you a potion. Something to take the edge off. Maybe a milk shake. I'm always in a better mood after I've had a milk shake."

"You tricked me with that worthless piece of glass."

"It was a crystal."

"It wasn't the stone!" she shrieked. "*I want the stone.*"

As if I wasn't panicked enough, I had

the stone in my handbag. Stupid, stupid, stupid Lizzy.

"Diesel has the stone," I said.

"I don't believe you. I think you're keeping it for yourself. You want the power of the stone."

"Honestly," I said. "The stone isn't all that powerful."

Nina crept up behind Anarchy and threw more powder at her. "Go away. Go away!"

Anarchy turned and glared at Nina. "You will die." And she set Nina's gown on fire.

Nina shrieked and ripped the gown off and ran out of the store. A piece of the gown set the feather boa display on fire, and in a flash, the entire front of the Exotica Shoppe was in flames.

"We need to get out of here," I said to Anarchy.

"There's no way out for you," she said. "You're going to die here. You're going to be consumed by the flames. And when you're dead, I'll find the stone."

"Look around you," I said. "You're going to die alongside me."

She smiled at me. “I can’t die. I have the power.”

She aimed the torch at me, and I batted it out of her hand. I shoved her out of my way, turned to run for the door, and Anarchy knocked me to my knees with a blow to the back of my head. I was trying to clear my head and shake it off, and the big free-standing set of shelves crashed down on me. There was instant pain in my leg and a wave of nausea. I tried to move, but I was pinned under the shelf.

I was surrounded by flames and choking on smoke. Anarchy had disappeared. I could hear the fire crackling and hissing around me. I yelled for help, but I doubted anyone could hear me. And I couldn’t imagine anyone being able to get through the flames to rescue me.

I had my arm across my face, trying to filter out the smoke as much as possible, and I felt the shelf lift off. It was Wulf. He tossed the shelf out of the way and knelt beside me.

“We’re even after this,” he said. “So stay alert. The next time we meet, I might not be this nice. Hatchet was able to remember most of the writing on the tablet . . . enough to make me believe I know where to find the next stone. I won't be happy if you try to prevent me from acquiring it."

He pulled me to my feet and wrapped his arms around me, holding me close, and that was the last I remember.

When I regained consciousness, I was on the ground across the street from the Exotica Shoppe. A paramedic was bending over me, offering oxygen. I sucked some in and sat up. Glo, Clara, and Nina were there. No Wulf.

"Where's Diesel?" I asked.

"He got here seconds after Wulf carried you out of the building. He made sure you were all right, and then he and Wulf went to look for Anarchy."

Glo, Clara, and Nina were smudged with soot. It was on their clothes, their arms, and their faces. Clara's hair had broken loose from its pins and was an electric mass of singed frizz. Nina was wrapped in a blanket, having left her gown inside the shop. They were all hovering over me, and I could see tear tracks streaking down their cheeks.

"We were so worried," Glo said, her voice breaking. "We tried to go back into the building to help you, but we couldn't get past the fire. It raced through the front of the store. The police and fire trucks came almost immediately, but if it hadn't been for Wulf . . ." She left off with a sob, brushed tears away, and wiped her nose on her sleeve.

"We don't even know how he got you out," Clara said. "He just appeared from behind a fire truck with you in his arms. He carried you across the street, and we all ran over to you. You weren't moving, and we were afraid . . ." Clara took a beat to get her composure. "Anyway, Wulf said you would be fine, and he didn't leave until the paramedic got to you. Diesel was here by then, too, and Wulf told Diesel he'd been following Anarchy. I guess that's how Wulf got to you so fast."

The paramedic tried to get me to my feet, but I had pain in my left leg, and I couldn't put my weight on it. He cut my jeans away at the knee, and I could see the swelling and the bruise developing midway between my knee and my ankle.

"Anarchy pushed one of the heavy display cases over and it fell on my leg," I said. "That's why I couldn't get out. I was trapped under the case. Wulf moved it off me, and the last thing I remember, he was holding me close with his arms wrapped around me."

"You should have your leg checked out," the paramedic said. "Let me stabilize it, and we'll get you to the ER."

I was waiting for the paramedic to return when Diesel crossed the street to me. "How are you doing?" he asked.

"I think my leg might be broken. They're going to take me in for an X ray. Did you find Anarchy?"

"Wulf and I tracked her down and trapped her in a blind alley. I was glad I had Wulf with me. It was like trying to capture a wild animal."

"What did you do with her?"

"We turned her over to the police."

"Will they be able to hold her?"

"Probably not. Apparently she's been losing the power she stole from Wulf, but she has her own arsenal of creepy, special abilities. One of which is being able to burn a handprint into flesh. She killed Reedy and threw him out the window when she discovered Wulf already had the book of sonnets."

"She told you that?"

"Yeah. She has a real anger management problem. She was ranting and babbling and foaming at the mouth while we were trying to capture her."

"Foaming at the mouth?"

"I made that up. I don't know why there was no record of her on file. I have a feeling she's been around for a while as Anarchy. And I think she's probably been looking for the stones at least as long as we have."

"And Wulf is regaining *his* power?"

"I don't know. Wulf and I don't spend a lot of time chatting."

The EMT rolled a stretcher over to me, and Diesel loaded me onto it.

"I haven't got my purse," I said to Diesel. "I don't have any of my medical insurance information."

"Where's your purse?"

"It was left in the building." I felt my heart stop for a beat. The SALIGIA Stone was in my purse.

"Oh boy," I said. "Bad news."

"Let me guess," Diesel said. "The stone was in your purse."

We looked across the street at the Exotica Shoppe. Not a lot left. Blackened brick walls. Most of the fire was out. What was left was smoldering rubble.

Three days later, Diesel helped me out of the car and handed me my crutches. I had a simple fracture. Surgery wasn't needed, but I'd be hobbling around for a while. Glo, Clara, and Nina were already on the sidewalk in front of what was left of the Exotica Shoppe. The yellow crime scene tape had been taken down, and the fire marshal had declared the area safe.

Everyone was wearing rubber boots and gloves, and I had a plastic garbage bag over my cast, held secure with electrician's tape. We all had rakes and shovels. We were going to look for the SALIGIA Stone.

"I'm so sorry about your shop," I said to Nina, "but I'm glad you weren't badly burned."

"Just some small burns on my hands from when I tore my gown off," Nina said. "I went home and put salve on them."

I looked at the gutted, blackened building. "There's not much left."

"Good riddance," Nina said. "I was over-insured. I'm going to rebuild something better. The truth is, this was a creaky, moldy old building. I'm going to put central air and a real pretty restroom in my new shop."

"Are you going to comb through this for salvageable items?" I asked her.

"Nope. Not worth it. It looks like mostly ashes to me. And I wouldn't want to give someone something that had been damaged by the heat. I've already put in an order for most everything, and I have a temporary location lined up." Nina waded into the debris. "You were over here in the corner, hiding behind the shelf. This must be where you dropped your purse."

We followed Nina and began picking through the rubble. We pushed charred jars and timbers away, and swept away ashes.

"I think I found something," Glo said. "I think this is the metal clasp on your shoulder bag."

We crowded around Glo, carefully pushed more ashes aside, and I was the first to see the little brown rock. I picked it up, and it hummed in my hand and gave off a brilliant blue aura.

"This is it," I said.

Everyone cheered.

"This is a happy ending," Nina said. "I'm going to the costume store to look for a new gown."

"I have an appointment at the hair salon," Clara said. "I'm going to get the singed ends trimmed off."

"And I have a date with the cute paramedic," Glo said. "I think he might be the one."

Diesel and I made our way back to his Aston Martin. He draped his arm across my shoulders and nuzzled my neck. "So what have we got here? Is this the True Love Stone or the Lust Stone?"

I slipped the stone into his jeans pocket. "There are some things a man should find out for himself."

ABOUT THE AUTHOR

JANET EVANOVICH is the #1 *New York Times* bestselling author of the Stephanie Plum novels, the Lizzy and Diesel novels, twelve romance novels, the Barnaby and Hooker novels and Trouble Maker graphic novels, and *How I Write: Secrets of a Bestselling Author*.

Visit Janet Evanovich's website at
www.evanovich.com
Facebook/JanetEvanovich

or

Write her at PO Box 2829
Naples, FL 34106